#GREY MATTERS

#GREY MATTERS

STEVEN LEE CLIMER

ISBN: 978-1-7379207-7-9 (Paperback)
ISBN: 978-1-7379207-8-6 (Hardcover)

Library of Congress Control Number: 2022934195

Any references to historical events, real people, or real places are used fictitiously. Names, characters, and places are products of the author's imagination.

Book design by Allison Chernutan.
Earth image by photographeeasia.

Printed in the United States of America.

First printing edition 2022.

emily@fracturedmirrorpublishing.com
Fractured Mirror Publishing
Knoxville, Tennessee

www.fracturedmirrorpublishing.com

I DEDICATE THIS NOVEL TO THE SUPPORT
OF MY NURSES AND DOCTORS AT THE
UNIVERSITY OF PENNSYLVANIA

EPIS⊙DE ONE

Meanwhile...

"*Come on in and have a seat.*"

Dylan looked around and pushed the dark hair out of his eyes. The professional who invited him to sit wore a polo shirt, and it was clear he kept in good shape. His arms stressed the sleeves, and his nipples were prominent beneath the fabric. Dylan put his backpack down at his feet.

"Dylan, right?" He smiled. Charming. Like a piranha. Very gummy. He wasn't as cute as Dylan thought initially. This man was a Monet; initially. He appeared hot, but upon closer inspection, he was not. "Thanks for coming. Please shut the door."

"Not like I had a choice," replied Dylan and did as he was instructed. He was also amazingly fit and lean, and he knew this doctor was drinking him in. "You said my scholarship could be in jeopardy if I didn't come in."

He nodded. "I'm Dr. Robert Bain."

7

"Okay, so that doesn't tell me anything."

Dr. Bain grinned, "A bit aggressive…" He flipped open a file and looked at some notations, "yes, I see that."

"I'm not aggressive. You called me in here, telling me my scholarship may be taken away. I'm not aggressive, I'm nervous. And you're looking in a file that's obviously about me."

"I can understand that," said Dr. Bain. "Dylan, do you like it here? The University? Do you like painting?"

"I love painting. I'd die if I couldn't paint." Dylan scanned the room, "What's going on?" Then he understood. "This is 'The Meeting,' isn't it?"

"It is," replied the doctor. "It's the meeting every person your age has. We have the results from your high school exit scan."

"I took that four months ago," said Dylan. "You're just now getting around to it?"

"Your case is a bit different because of your artistic talents."

"I don't understand."

"Let me explain it to you, then." Dr. Bain hesitated and flexed a little too obviously. "I do know you are gay, and that you do like older guys. But that's beside the point."

"Surveillance? How is digging into my personal life related to any of this test shit?"

"When the results of the test reveal a lapse in grey matter of between six and ten percent in the temporal pole, we are allowed, by law, to do a background check."

"You're saying I have less grey matter in the temporal pole? What does that even mean?"

"It means you are strongly predisposed to psychopathic behavior, or development of psychopathic or sociopathic later in life. The test is accurate into the 90th percentile of prediction."

"Wait a minute, because of a brain scan you are telling me I am a psychopath?"

Dr. Bain grinned nervously. "You're oversimplifying it."

"Well maybe I need it simplified so I can understand it. Up to ten percent of my brain is missing."

"Aggression. Frustration." Dr. Bain leaned in. "Do you have homicidal thoughts?"

"This is nuts," Dylan got up and grabbed his backpack. "I need to get to class."

"Sit down. We need to finish the meeting. It is my opinion alone that can make or break this for you."

"And I suppose you want me to suck your cock to get on your good side?" Dylan sat back down. "Or do you want me to fuck you?"

"Dylan…" Dr. Bain dangled his words, "there are a lot of things that can be done. It depends on your answers. And cooperation."

"Are you now going to tell me my options?"

"I can, but I want to first go over a few things in your file." He opened the folder and pulled out some photographs. "Can you tell me about these paintings? They're stunning, but a little unsettling."

Dylan pulled one over so he could better see it. "I love this one. It's what got me into art school." He studied the abstract of a silhouetted woman walking through rain and lightning. "It's about perseverance."

Dr. Bain nodded. "Okay, what about the other ones?"

Dylan gave them a quick scan. "They're all mine. I know them well. They are a part of me. You're asking me to explain my soul? This is really stupid. Can I go now?"

"Antisocial and aggressive."

"Stop saying that. I'm not any of those things. I'm very social. And I am not aggressive."

Dr. Bain slid over another piece of paper. "Can you explain this? It's an arrest for failure to follow a police officer's orders."

Dylan laughed. "I was fifteen and on my bike. I got off the street because a car was coming, and a cop told me to get off the sidewalk. There was dangerous traffic. So, I said no, it's not safe. I didn't fight with him."

"You disobeyed his authority."

"It was thrown out in court by the judge. Or isn't that in there?" Dylan leaned back in his chair. "Of course, it isn't in there because I was a minor and it was sealed. Then it was expunged because it was thrown out by the judge. So, how many more mistakes and errors are in there?"

"Careful of your attitude, Dylan." He closed the file. "Do you know what I can do here? I have two options: I can order a retest and file an affidavit stating your creativity and artistic contributions to our society would be greatly hampered by recommending corrective procedure."

"What's corrective procedure?" Dylan's blood chilled. "That doesn't sound good."

"It's good for someone with your test results because it can correct the deficient grey matter by replacing it with genetically-reproduced or donated grey matter."

"Brain surgery? But there's nothing wrong with me."

"The test says otherwise. It's a preventative measure, and it's perfectly legal here in the United States. The procedure has corrected others with your deficiency, and they have gone on to live uneventful lives."

"Uneventful? Because you did something to their brains?" Dylan stood up. "I want to talk to my parents."

"They have nothing to do with this. You're over 18. You're not a minor. And this law is mandatory." Dr. Bain sighed. "I'm not trying to make this difficult, Dylan. I like you. I think you have a lot of potential."

"That you want to erase by putting in extra grey matter? That's fucking nuts."

"You will need to stop swearing."

"You need to stop threatening my life."

"I am not threatening your life. I'm saving your life. And those around you." He sighed, frustrated. "Do you remember the insanity of anti-vaxxers a few years ago? And how many kids died because parents weren't vaccinating them? Remember when mumps caused over 50 miscarriages in New York City alone because the teacher in a prenatal class was an anti-vaxxer and her five-year-old son infected the entire class? Most of those babies died. The others had birth defects."

"I don't have the mumps."

"You're missing the point. We must protect the herd from psychotic and sociopathic people. Too many get guns or go on serial-killing sprees."

"That is the most insane straw man fallacy I have ever heard. Ever think of stopping people from getting guns instead of doing brain surgery on them?"

"I'm sorry you don't get it. You don't have to. This is the law."

"Do you have all your grey matter?" asked Dylan.

"This is about you," replied Dr. Bain. "I think I'm ready to make my recommendation."

"What's it going to say?"

Dr. Bain took a deep breath, measuring and picking his words before letting them fall out of his mouth. "Do you think we could come to a conclusion together?"

"I can tell you what I want the recommendation to be." Dylan said. He considered the doctor's intense blue eyes and pecs. "I want no one to bother me ever again. What do I have to do for that to happen? Will that set me free?"

"Yes, I will fix your results so no one will ever bother you again. I want you to just sit back and let me take care of you. Completely. I'd do all the work and you will feel amazing."

"What do you want to do to me?" Inconspicuously, Dylan unzipped the bag sitting beside his seat. "Do you want to go down on me?"

"Yes."

"Do you want eat my ass?"

"Oh yes."

Dylan smiled. "You're a sick bastard, aren't you?"

"I think you are, too," said Dr. Bain. "I have your surveillance. I know what you've been doing and watching online. I think this will work out well for both of us."

"What did you see—that I looked at—that you liked too?"

"Daddy sites. Daddies that were beefy or ripped or hairy. Daddies with twinks."

"You think I'm a twink?"

"Oh, no, not at all. I didn't mean to offend you." His demeanor switched. "I'd never say that about you. You're in charge. I really want to make you happy, Dylan."

"First, stop saying my name. It's disgusting." He reached in his bag and pulled out a white pistol. "Did you read anything else other than my porn preferences?"

Dr. Bain shot back in his seat, pointing at the gun. "You can't have that. How did you get that in here? We have metal detectors."

"You'd know that if you looked at some of my searches, and what I'm studying in class. Ever hear of 3D printing? Plastic guns? Oh, and I know all about the test. You may do yourself a favor and stop thinking young people who are brain scanned are stupid. I'm not. I'm brilliant. I'm talented. And I came prepared."

"Did you know your scan would be positive?"

"No, but I was going to make sure I didn't disappear like at least ten of the kids I went to high school with did, or the two guys out of my dorm, too." He cocked the gun. "All after having 'The Meeting.'"

"What are you going to do?" Dr. Bain squirmed. "You've sealed your fate. You're going to go to prison for doing this. This is murder, or attempted murder."

Dylan stood up. "No, it's murder. Put your hands up and slide your chair back against the wall. I don't want you to be able to call for help." He laughed as he saw the doctor sweating. "I bet your boner is gone like a little turtle."

"You can't get out of here. They'll catch you."

"I came in here thinking only one of us would come out of this meeting. I have had friends vanish after their test. I wanted to be prepared in the event you wanted to incarcerate me against my will if things turned bad. I personally don't care if I don't, but I am determined to make sure you can't do this to anyone anymore. I think it's a worthy sacrifice."

"You are a psychopath."

"Oh, and one more thing." Dylan tapped a small camera that inconspicuously looked like a button on his shirt. "This is going out to the Internet. So even if you somehow get out of this, everyone heard you. Pervert. I'm sure there's a brain scan for that, right?"

"Everyone will know you murdered me. Did you think about that when you decided to broadcast it?"

"I didn't think that far ahead, but I am fucked no matter what, right? I would rather go down as a hero taking out a sick asshole like you out and go to jail. They will experiment on me one way or another."

"Fuck you, asshole. I should have just signed the papers when I first got them."

"But you thought you could get me to fuck you first, right?" Dylan laughed. He pointed the gun at Dr. Bain's crotch. "First shot here? Or in your head?"

"You're sick."

"I'm giving you the choice now. I'm sure we can come up with a conclusion together. That's what you said."

"You're not going to shoot me," Dr. Bain made a small motion towards the phone. "And if that camera is live, someone is going to report this and come any minute."

Dylan laughed. "Don't you know psychopaths and sociopaths are liars. It's in our missing grey matter. I never said it was a live feed. You don't know anything."

"I'm calling for help." Dr. Bain reached for the phone.

Dylan squeezed off one shot. It was a muffled pop like a firecracker. Just a singular, crack that would go unnoticed by anyone who may have heard it. Dylan specifically selected the blueprints for a 3D plastic gun that was the quietest available—on the dark web.

The bullet smashed through Dr. Bain's penis and pelvis. The

bones were no match for the plastic bullet designed to cause maximum damage. The doctor didn't scream, but the realization that Dylan wasn't bluffing reflected in his eyes. His pants turned red.

"Do you believe the test results now?" Dylan put the gun against Dr. Bain's forehead. "I think this is the location of grey matter, right?"

"Please…"

"You're done hurting people."

He pulled the trigger; and Dylan found this small measure of justice truly scrumptious.

A hot, dry breeze ruffled the white linen sheets of the hotel room. Phineas Fletcher had been up since dawn, but his roommates were still unconscious. They would no doubt have questions about how they all came to be in Ibiza when they woke. He consulted the aperture on his wrist. Why the hell he ever invented it, Phineas couldn't recall at present. He should be using the aperature to find out what was happening to all the people in his sphere of influence: Carmen, PJ, the boys, Calliope. If he let his guard down, the responsibilities on his shoulders would crush him into the ground, then step on him with spiked high heels, for good measure.

In the bed, Nash stirred. He was wrapped in fine French bedsheets. Instinctively, he reached over to see if he was alone. A smile crossed his lips as he caressed the muscular naked torso of Ray. His skin felt warm and dry; Nash was the only person aside from Kendall who could actually touch the skin of Ray Kellen.

"Ah, you're awake," said Fletcher.

The sound of his boss' voice in the room was unexpected, Nash sat up. "What are you doing in here?" Then he looked around, "And where is here?"

"We are in a safe house in Ibiza. After the confrontation with Calliope and the subsequent thermo-nuclear explosion, we were ejected into the sea. Thankfully, it seems as if Ray's shield protected us from dying."

"Wait," Nash rubbed his beard and face to wake up. "What?"

Ray opened one eye and looked at them. "Could you guys be any louder? I'm still sleeping."

You can keep sleeping, Princess, but I had to talk to you before leaving." Fletcher had gotten their attention. "I have to get some answers because everything is going to shit really fast. I waited long enough."

"What are you talking about?" asked Nash, fully awake now.

"Get up, I have to give you something," stated Fletcher.

Nash could see he was quite serious and rolled out of the sheets. He only had on underwear. Ray scooted up to a sitting position but remained in the bed. Fletcher held the aperture up to his eyes and looked at all the strange whirring cogs, wheels, and flashing mechanical pieces turning.

"You're ready for this," said Fletcher.

"What?" Nash stood. "This is unexpected."

"Why?"

"I...I...I don't feel ready for it."

Fletcher smiled, "That's why you are. You used to be so indignant and thought you deserved it. As a Scholar, your brain and experience are your best attributes, and an aperture just helps you reach all the goals you have." Fletcher took it off his wrist and closed the few steps that separated them. "Hold out your wrist."

Fletcher strapped the leather band around Nash's wrist. The aperture then made a few strange noises Nash had never heard before, the dials and cogs spinning wildly.

"What's it doing?" asked Nash.

"It's calibrating itself to you—so it can serve you."

"That's so fucking awesome," commented Ray from the bed.

Nash exhaled and grinned. "Wow, I can physically feel its weight. But," he touched his chest, "I can feel it in here. And I can hear it in my mind."

"It has accepted you," said Fletcher. "Makes me feel good about its new master."

Ray got up out of bed, dragging bedsheets wrapped around his waist. "I want to see it." He took Nash's wrist. "That is so cool. Professor, who made these things? I mean, they all look so old."

Fletcher sighed, realizing he could no longer keep his deepest secrets—at least from these two. "I did. I made all six of the apertures that are in existence."

"You?" Nash looked confused. "I'm not following. I thought you're a Scholar. I didn't know you invented as well."

"A lot of Scholars are inventors," said Fletcher. "I just happen to have a knack for manipulating time, the Veil, etcetera."

Then Ray paused, thinking. "If you are giving it to him, how are you getting back home. What's going on?"

"You're perceptive even without your oracle." Fletcher walked over to the bright windows and closed just one of the room-darkening curtains. Long shadows from the furniture and doorways stained the carpet. "I have other ways I can travel."

"Where are you going?" asked Nash.

"I have to see my father and find out a few things: namely what happened to PJ and Carmen. I'm sure I will think of some more things for him. He owes me a few answers, to be honest."

"Who is you father?" asked Ray.

"Pluto."

The room was silent.

"I'm sorry, did you say Pluto? God of the Underworld?"

Fletcher nodded. "That's another long story, but yes, he is my father."

"Does that make you a….a…god?"

"Yes, family always has drama, right?" He laughed at his own attempt at humor. "My mother was murdered by an early version of the Wire, but that's yet another story for another day."

"Wow, I'm sorry. Those bastards," said Ray. "Can you do anything? You know, like my shield or Calliope's energy ball thing?"

"I can do some things, but it is my personal networking that is most important."

"I don't understand," said Ray.

"I have become acquaintances, good friends, with a lot of post-human entities."

"Post-human, I like that." Ray laughed. "I'm post-human."

"Is there anything I can do to help you?" asked Nash, realizing the gravity of his promotion.

"No, not yet. Just keep everything from blowing up while I'm gone." They watched curiously as Fletcher angled the bathroom door to create a long shadow across the floor. "Okay, I think this will work. I am out of here for now. Remember, don't blow up the world. That comes later."

Fletcher stood in the shadow, crossed his arms, and fell backward into it as if it were a pool of black, fathomless water. Then he was gone.

Ray grabbed Nash by the wrist. "What just happened?"

"The son of the god of the Underworld just went home. I'm pretty sure that's what happened."

There was a long silence as they watched the shadow for any movement. When they realized nothing else was going to happened, they let out a collective sigh.

"When do we have to go?" asked Ray.

Nash smiled, his eyes twinkling. "We don't have to go right away." He pulled Ray closer, cupping his hand behind his neck, and steered Ray's lips towards his. "There is still time for this."

Dolce unfurled her mermaid tail against the warm rocks of the northern Orkneyjar Island coast. Englishmen called it Orkney, but the Norse called it Orkneyjar. It was not the main island in the Scottish archipelago—Dolce sprawled out on the rocky outcropping of the hidden island, Forntida gud hem, which roughly translated into 'ancient god island.'

The sun was bright and it was unusually warm, and Dolce

stretched, enjoying it. She could not be out of the water long, and it wasn't for breathing purposes. Air dried out her scales; sometimes they would crack, just like any creature with dried out flesh.

There was so much energy in the village because of the arrival of the Girl. She was mysterious, indeed, but she was brought to them by the Ancient One himself: Cthulhu. Dolce was sure she had a name, and she would reveal it in time, when she woke up. But she had been asleep for over a week. The mermaid was unconcerned. She was not in the circle of the priests and priestesses that served the Ancient One, but Dolce knew him intimately from swimming with him. He was terrifying but seemed to let her be even though he could crush her with one tentacle if he wanted.

As Dolce drank in the tinkling sunshine dancing on the water, three large black birds landed silently on the rocks in front of her. With her hand, she shielded her eyes to get a better look at them. Their eyes blinked rapidly, flashing, and they clicked their beaks at her.

"Hi there, you want to soak up the sun too?" She leaned up on her elbows, shook her long reddish-brown hair, and looked at them with her aquamarine eyes. "Plenty of room."

The birds, though, were agitated. Suddenly, the two outside birds savagely pecked at the chest of the middle one. They shrieked and screamed as feathers and blood covered the rocks. Aghast, Dolce could only look on in shock. The blood spilled out onto the rock followed by entrails. Then the middle bird fell dead.

"Oh my god!"

Dolce rose up to a kneeling position and stared at the garish scene. The two live birds looked at her and gave several long caws. There was an image in the guts: sinews made shapes, dark blood and feathers suggested a face. It was the Girl, and her eyes were open.

"She's awake."

The birds then covered their dead sibling with their wings,

who, in the hidden recess, became whole again. Then they flew off. Dolce knew a divination when she saw one. They must be the oracles for the Girl. Indeed, she was a god, and this would put all the speculation to rest.

Dolce closed her eyes and concentrated. Slowly, the scales of her lower half absorbed into her body, leaving behind human flesh and wobbly legs. She stood, wrapped herself in a light fabric shawl and began to walk towards the village.

The walk wasn't far, but it was taxing on the mermaid. Summoning legs required a lot of bloodstream magic and walking on them was even worse. Magic did not assist with walking; Dolce was on her own. She was not a big fan of human legs, but she needed them to periodically journey inland when summoned or, in this case, investigating a divination.

As she arrived in the tiny village made up of rustic cabins on stilts, Dolce was greeted with the reverence she deserved. The humans called her mermaid, but she was a selkie. The Celts roughly translated that to Seal Person. A selkie could sing, mesmerizing men and creatures alike. Selkie songs could also make the weather do her bidding—hence a sunny warm day in the Orkney Islands.

"She's here," whispered one of the attendant priests to another as Dolce entered the small cabin where the Girl was sleeping. "It's her. It's the Selkie."

"Where is Nolanne?" asked Dolce. "I received a divination." One attendant simply pointed to a small back bedroom with a closed door. "Thank you."

Dolce glided in silent grace to the door and opened it. Inside, she saw that the Girl was still unconscious in the bed. Her face was covered with bruises and burns, but they seemed to be healing quickly. The first thought that came to mind was how the Ancient One came to rescue this unremarkable human girl, a child really, and deposit her in the village of his followers?

"Lady Dolce, what a surprise to see you here." Nolanne went to the Selkie and gave a slight curtsey of respect.

Dolce considered Nolanne pensively. She did not like her at all. Nolanne couldn't hide her emotions from a Selkie, no human could. However, the Ancient One spoke to Nolanne and gave her direction on what he desired. She was the perfect pawn for him: never a complaint, always pure blind devotion.

"I came as soon as I could," said Dolce. "I received a divination from this girl's oracle."

"Her oracle?" whispered Nolanne rhetorically. "Are you sure?"

"I do not usually confuse three birds who tear each others' innards out in front of me as anything else."

Nolanne lowered her head, "I am sorry, I did not mean to offend you, Lady Dolce."

Dolce sighed. She wanted to say *give it a rest you ass-kisser*, but she demurred. "None taken."

Dolce went to the Girl. She was so fair and pretty, but trouble made lines in her forehead. She inspected the wounds and wondered what caused them. Dolce placed her cool hand on the girl's forehead. She concentrated to aid her in comfort. And although she could not heal the flesh, a Selkie could ease the mind.

"Do you think she will wake soon?" asked Nolanne.

"I don't know, but in the divination, she was awake," replied Dolce. "There is a storm inside her head. I will try to help her ease it, but this one is volatile. I don't question the Ancient One's wisdom, but I wonder why he has selected this one for us to care for."

Dolce stood away from the unconscious girl. "Keep a close eye on her. Make a poultice of lichen and apply it to her forehead constantly. Do not let it get beyond body temperature and keep it moist."

"Yes, my Lady."

"Summon me when she wakes, but do not agitate her. I fear she may be dangerous if not handled carefully." Dolce made for the door. "I will try to find some answers if I can."

With those directives, Dolce left the village. She walked back to the rocks. The sun was no longer visible. A bitter wind descended with dense clouds, and an icy mist hung in the air. Proper weather for Forntida gud hem. Dolce's tail returned, consuming the human legs that she detested so. Then the Selkie slipped from the rocks and into the chilly protected bay.

In the water, Dolce was fierce. She was a quick as a seal and darted around the sharp rocks and submerged hazards of the wrecked boats of men who dared try to come ashore. Fortina gud hem was sacred and was not kind to strangers. Dolce dove deep into the inky blackness, her brilliant aquamarine eyes could see perfectly in the din.

Finally, she came to the surface in a small secluded bay on the far side of the island where tall white cliffs towered with silent intimidation over the water. On the main face of the white limestone, the followers of the Ancient One had cleaved a vertical surface upon which a great stone carving of Cthulhu loomed. His cephalopod head with myriad of writhing tentacles glared down from the rock. The carving was never allowed to become worn or faded, and caretakers were constantly restoring any blemish to its pristine origin.

This was the place for the most sacred ceremonies of the Ancient One. Over the centuries, numerous sacrifices took place on the stone altars below the carving. Dolce never understood why a god would need the devotion of such tiny, insignificant souls. To the Ancient One, they must seem like krill to a feeding whale shark. He would have to eat enormous amounts of them to get any satisfaction, and to Dolce that just seemed like too much work. It was not for her to understand it, though.

Dolce hoped there would be some clues as to what was transpiring with the Girl. If there were, it would surely be at this altar where Cthulhu would show to claim his tributes. There was nothing, though, not even workers tending to the sculpture. Momentarily, Dolce paused to look at the immense sheer wall of rock. Workers dangled from precarious ropes to constantly tend to the giant image of the Ancient One. It loomed over the simple stone altar surrounded by stones that resembled Stonehenge. Soon it would be filled with acolytes and followers hoping to see their god claim this child.

Across the world, in another place and time, someone else was waking. Carmen Perez fussed in her childhood bed in a small town fifty miles from Matamoros, Mexico—just south of the U.S. border. She sat up in her bed, rubbing her eyes in disbelief. Perhaps she was still dreaming. The sheets were Pokémon; the walls were pink; even her unicorn lamp on her white desk was there.

Vision.

She had vison. Carmen went to the small mirror on her desk and looked at her face. She was nine again, not a woman. Dark hair, a smattering of freckles over her nose that her family always teased her about—a Latina girl with freckles, like a redhead. Carmen liked them and smiled. Around the mirror were photos and cards taped to the frame. She found one of her bestie, Selena. They used to sing Selena songs together whenever they did anything together.

Nine, how strange. What a specific place in time in which to dream. It was the happiest time of her life, and just before she started losing her sight. Then, her stomach sank. The happiest period in her life ended with the worst day in her life. It was the day her parents and brother were murdered.

No, please. Don't make me see it again.

Carmen heard the familiar sobs. Forlorn tears, grief, unspeakable loss.

I can't do this again.

The sobs became a tragic wail. Carmen knew what was going to happen. In her mind, she remembered everything that happened with Nemesis and the power she now commanded. The universe blessed her with its most potent power, she was the Hammer. Maybe she could change the outcome. Let the bastards come.

Outside, the sound of several vehicles pulled up to the house. Carmen went to the window and looked out at the collection of SUVs and trucks that belonged to the local drug cartel. One of them was shouting at the front of the house.

"Manuel, *necesitamos hablar contigo!*"

We need to talk to you!

They did not want to talk to her father. They came to kill him—the local mayor who dared fight back against the cartel for the people of his town. Other men got out of their vehicles.

She heard her father go out on the front porch and address them in Spanish: "I have no quarrel with you. We just want to live as a town in peace. This is your town, too. Please, respect that. This is all our home."

"That is a warm sentiment," said the drug lord, "but you are a threat to our money. Our business. There are two options. Work with us or be removed as the roadblock you are being."

"I am the mayor—duly elected—to represent our town. To make it better. Do you not want it better? Just keep your operations out of town."

"You cannot tell us what to do," a gun was cocked and aimed at him. "You don't run things, I do."

In the past, this was the moment her father was gunned down. The instant that her mother was raped and murdered. This heartbeat when her brother was shot dead. This time, though, time froze. The very air stopped moving. Around her mother's flowers, the bees were suspended in mid-air.

Carmen looked beyond the vehicles and men who stood suspended in time to a woman in a white wedding dress behind them. She wore a veil covering her face, and she was sobbing. Carmen knew her; it was not the first time La Llorona visited.

"Please, help me La Llorona. Don't let them kill my family again."

There was no answer. The figure moved like vapor over the

hot dirt. The sobs became a wail, La Llorona's song of misery. She paused when she got between the men and the porch stairs where Carmen stood.

"*Por favor.*"

La Llorona lifted her veil, revealing a countenance of sugar skull. "The power has come to you, like I told you it would years ago. It is why I saved you from these evil creatures the first time."

"But my eyesight, why did you take it from me?"

"I did not. The bloodstream flows through us all and you are the Hammer now. The Hammer must be blind and not tempted by the lies of the eyes. Human eyes are so easily fooled."

"Do you know what's happened to me?"

La Llorona nodded. "I know all. I have brought you here to center you. Give you the task you were born to complete. You are the Hammer. You can equalize. You can avenge. Take revenge. Wield the Bloodstream. Destroy the enemies of the weak, the unfortunate, the different."

"But my father said revenge and vengeance were evil in and of themselves. A beast that once tasted blood would not be controlled. Couldn't be controlled."

"Shall we watch what happened to your father—again?"

"No, please." Tears streamed down the little girl's face. "Can I save them?"

"No, the past has already taken place. But I have given you this opportunity to see what the Hammer can do. You can go forth and be the weapon of justice."

"But how?"

Atacar!

"I am afraid," confessed Carmen. "I don't know how to strike at my enemies. I thought I could, many times, but Nemesis took over and saved me. She can do it."

Mentirosa!

"She is not a liar," said Carmen. "She saved me."

"She saved you to save herself. To come back in your body."

A smile cracked her sugar lips, "You took care of that, though. You exiled her and now you control all of the bloodstream's retribution. You are the Hammer." La Llorona raised one hand nonchalantly. "Perhaps, direct threat will be able to steel your nerve."

Time came alive again. The bees buzzed about the blossoms and the men aimed their guns. Screaming, Carmen grabbed her head like she was keeping it from exploding. The ribbons of energy shot up out of the ground from beneath the men, impaling them on spikes of pinkish purple cabers. They instantly solidified into black, shiny obsidian stone, impaling the men. Even their vehicles were lifted into the air and spiked.

La Llorona lowered her veil. "Now you know how to do it."

"What do I do now?"

"Wake up."

Then the specter faded to vapor in the hot Mexican sun of her dreams.

EPISDE TWO

Burn Your House Down

Kendall's sleep was lucid, dancing, shapes, colors. Fragrances he'd never known filled his senses to the brim. Intoxication, the drowsy drunk feeling was there even when asleep. In his mind, replaying over and over, was the birth of the creature that now was virtually inseparable from him. The baby planet had surely attached to him deeply.

"Kendall, wake up." Poppy kicked at his foot.

"What, PJ? I'm sleeping. I need my beauty sleep. It's hard looking this good."

She sighed, "It's not PJ, dumbass. It's me. Now wake up. We need you. The baby needs you."

The baby?

That's right, there was a baby—a baby planet that was born in his lap in the Pierian Spring. He popped up.

"What's up?"

"While you have been sleeping here in a bed of roses, the baby's been anxious and, well, there have been some developments."

"Like what kind of developments?"

"I think it's best to show you."

Without further words, Poppy led Kendall through the soft meadow where he slept. The witches, servants of Mother Earth, afforded Kendall every luxury so he could recuperate from all that he did.

It wasn't far and they arrived in a grotto of wisteria and honeysuckle that draped from a stone pergola. Beneath the fragrant vines, rested a soft, pink, round thing—in essence a fleshy blob to Kendall—and it pulsed with a gentle rainbow aura. As he got closer, the glow intensified.

"Hey, there," he softly said. "You look a little different from the last time I saw you."

Just then, the graceful red reptilian Etienne joined them. "She is growing. And she seems to like you."

"Well, who wouldn't. I mean, this hair. This face." He grinned.

"Gross," said Poppy. "I just threw up in my mouth a little bit."

Kendall ignored her. "A *she*, huh? So, what's up? I was hoping to get back soon."

"You will in due time," said Etienne, eyes blinking vertically. "We think there is something she may be trying to tell us. We cannot do a proper goddess divination, and we ask you to see if there is something you can see."

"Okay, it won't hurt, will it? Those divinations are no joke."

"I can't promise…"

Kendall sighed. The blob didn't look too dangerous. He could feel the energy, the bond between them. Kendall approached and knelt on the soft moss of the grotto and raised an apprehensive hand to touch her. He knew he shouldn't hesitate; he knew this creature, was there at her birth. Still, the unknown was just beneath his fingertips.

Suddenly, there was a surge in the glow. A hand emerged, slender and pale, and reached for Kendall's. He didn't resist and accepted the gentle, silky hand into his.

I have something to show you.

He heard the voice but couldn't see the face. Around him were Poppy, Etienne, and the other attendants. None of them seemed to see the hand coming from within the entity, or the subsequent embrace.

Come inside. I have to show you things.

"Hey, did you hear that?" said Kendall aloud as an open invitation. "Seriously, what are you people doing? Don't you see this?"

Poppy sharpened her eyes at him. "We don't see anything but you with your hand out."

"Wait," said Etienne. "He is having a divination."

"I have never seen a divination like this in all my days," said Poppy.

"I am not sure an oracle has ever had this much direct access before," said Etienne. Then she spoke louder: "Kendall, what do you see?"

"I'm holding hands with a baby planet! She says I have to go inside so she can show me things. What do I do?"

"Fuck, dipshit!" shouted Poppy. "Go!"

Kendall let the aura pull him closer. The world's noise became stillness. Seduced, he lowered his head ever closer to the surface. He could smell so many different things: roses, decay, his mother's perfume.

Small ripples swelled and took on shapes. A baby hippo turned to consider his face then sank beneath the surface. Then in a magnificent tango played a perfect soundtrack to the shapes that rose marched, in front of Kendall, and dissipated on the other side.

A tropical island beach lapped by the sea's tongue.
Ray.
Nash.
The great pyramid at Giza.

Mona Lisa.
A shark frenzy.
A writhing gyre of baby garter snakes.
PJ.

Kendall gasped, "PJ? Is that you?"

The shape seemed to respond to his voice. It softened and PJ's familiar smirk was there.

"Where are you? I need to see you. We've been so worried."

The face, however, did not answer and was swallowed like a melting ball of ice cream, back into the surface.

"Hello?" Kendall heard the woman's fragile voice speak. "I think you are looking for me."

"Who said that?" said Kendall. "Show me!"

In the next blink of his eye, Kendall was no longer in the grotto. He descended like he was tethered to a parachute, but when he looked up it was only blue skies. The ground was coming up fast, and he barely had time to react before smashing onto a beach. Kendall stood. The bright sun off the sea was blinding.

"Who's there?" he demanded.

"It's me," said the woman's voice again.

Wiping the sweat from his eyes, Kendall tried his best to render meaning to the shapes. Someone was surely walking towards Kendall in the visage of heat mirages that danced on the hot sand. At first, it was PJ but then as the shape moved, he thought it was Carmen. Each step of the mirage confounded his senses. Then, as if from behind a sheer curtain walked a person Kendall did not know.

"Who are you?" he asked.

"I'm Allison."

He studied her and found that she wasn't pretty, but not yet ugly. He settled on basic. "Have we met before?"

"I'm a little too old to run with your crowd, sorry. I am this little planet's oracle."

Kendall grinned, "Wow, that is so cool. She's a baby goddess. Ooh, that would be a great t-shirt." Then he paused. "Wait, I thought I was the oracle."

"You are a strong oracle, yes. You are an oracle to another god but were able to find me. You know who I am now so please come find me and get me back here."

"I don't know who you are. You just told me your name and told me you are the baby's oracle even though I'm doing the oracle-ing right here, right now, just fine."

"We thank you for that, honestly." She stepped closer. "Even though I am a version of Allison, and I was sent to greet you, the present-tense Allison has no idea of what is going on. She is lost, and she is in great, great danger. You must find her for me. I trust you."

"Where is she?"

But there was no answer. The aura dimmed; Kendall was pushed out of the mirage and back into reality. He stood over the baby planet's pupae case, wondering what just happened. He was about to turn around and ask if anyone else saw the things he did, but a face began to swell out of the pupae. It was fair, unspeakably beautiful—the kind of face that caused chaos. Then, a compulsion that he could not fight overcame Kendall. He lowered his lips, at her mercy, and let her kiss him. It was not a kiss of passion, but of hope. Information transferred. Images of a great tragedy that was about to happen. They had to save Allison who was about to die a horrible death.

Kendall broke the kiss and shook his head to get his thinking straight. "Guys, we have a huge problem. I was just shown the baby planet's oracle, but we have to find her, like now. She is about to die."

Etienne stepped forth, "Tell me everything."

"Okay, first," Kendall smiled as he looked upon the infant planet, "her name is Betty."

She kept her head down as she walked onto the subway train at City Hall in Philly. It was midday, mid-week, mid-summer, she couldn't keep it straight. The train was light of passengers. She heard the voice overhead say doors are closing.

What was her name? Sometimes she thought she could remember. If she looked at her paperwork from the doctors it would have her name on it. But was that really her? That person was dead as far as she remembered.

She did remember a boy from her dreams. He was young and handsome with blonde hair. She knew him even though she'd never met him. Perhaps it was just a fantasy, the hope of having one normal thing in her life again.

Things looked different on the other side of a coma. Three months out from a shocking brain aneurism, and she was only now getting back out into the world. It wasn't as if she didn't want to go out in public, but the world was so very raw. Not the world, just the people. The overhead voice repeated: doors are closing. Then, they indeed closed.

There could be no eye contact—at least not with grown-ups. They were the most different. Animals looked the same; babies did, too. However, she noticed that at about age seven, people started changing. Mostly for the worst. She could see it in their faces, their eyes, the slope of their foreheads, the way their ears hung. They cast glances at her, and watched her from the reflections. Perhaps, they could always see what she had never seen up until recently. After the coma. The sleep that left her with extra vision.

Sounds remained the same. There was nothing hiding in the waves or frequencies of a person's voice, or the song on the radio. She had taken to wearing headphones to avoid accidental contact that may lead to having to look at someone's face. She didn't want to see that truth. Not anymore.

Upon waking, the nurses looked different than she remembered. Not just the nurses but all the people. Doctors, housekeeping, even her mother had a quality of clarity in their faces when she looked at them that disturbed her. The therapists, both mental and physical, had the clarity quality, too. She hated it. The true face of people was visible to her. She couldn't think of another way to describe this clarity when she saw people. It was their true faces, unhidden. Why did her coma leave this burden behind? She was happier with a person's false face.

Only the second time back out in public, she found a seat on the train. Still, she kept her head down. She didn't want to see their faces, couldn't bear to see their faces. The doctor said she had to get out, and she couldn't stay in forever. His face was melted. One eye scarred over with skin, and the other foggy with cataracts. She kept her reactions in check after the first time she told about seeing her doctor's true face.

The therapist followed. His face, too, was full of raw truth. His flesh was translucent snow with blue veins circling his eyes. And a serpent's forked tongue darted when he talked. They told her to speak up when she was having hallucinations, or some other possible mental issue, in order to determine the depth of the damage she would have to live with.

When she first described what she saw, not just in him but in everyone, the medications followed. The neurologist had the face of a fish that gasped for air constantly. The psychiatrist had large open nostrils with small tendrils undulating as if in an underwater current. Only the housekeeper was tolerable to look at; she had four arms and the face of an angel with pink wings. However, all of them told her it was just her imagination, a side-effect of her trauma, an affliction that would fade with time.

The pharmaceuticals helped for a while. She wasn't afraid because everyone said the hallucinations were part of her recovery. Most faces were acceptably dull with minor distortions. Her health had returned as did most of her faculties. It was only after she was released from the hospital and recovering at home that she realized the truth. People wore masks. They hid who they really were. Not from her, though. The true faces were unavoidable. She began to know people by their shoes and their voices. The psychiatrist became brown loafers. The angel-faced housekeeper, Converse.

It was all different now. She rode the train back from her last meeting with the doctors, and one last brain scan. They were worried about something after the accident, something that they thought would get better with time. Other patients had gotten better, but she had not. Her grey matter around her temporal pole was reduced by eight percent. There was concern in their monstrous faces. None of them could hide from her.

She looked down at the far end of the car. Coming through the doors separating the cars, a homeless woman emerged. To others she was a homeless woman. To her, she was an elegant, long-necked creature with red flesh. On the top of her long, graceful neck was a tiny head with great green snake eyes. Vertical slits locked on her. Then there was the smile.

She was locked in place, unable to move as the woman glided down the aisle. Others looked at her. They turned their heads or put on their sunglasses. Most had headphones on so they could ignore her if she talked to them. However, this creature had no interest in any of them. She kept coming down the aisle until she reached her destination.

"What is your name?" The woman said, blinking her eyes vertically rather than horizontally.

"I don't remember."

"You know it. It is alright to say it."

"I don't know who I am now."

"Who were you, before you could see the truth?"

"Allison. I was Allison."

"Allison, the girl who sees the truth." The eyes blinked. "Are you afraid of me?"

"No. I'm used to the hallucinations. It's part of my illness. I mean, a part of my injury." Allison looked at her. "Who are you?"

"Etienne," she replied.

"That is a beautiful name."

"Thank you."

"Are you going to hurt me?" asked Allison. "I don't mind if you do. I'm tired."

"I understand, but I am not here to hurt you. I could never hurt someone who could see the truth."

"What do you mean?"

Etienne turned Allison towards her reflection in the subway car window. They zipped along, concrete supports and lights strobing by. Allison looked no different than she always had. Etienne, who stood by her, looked like a graceful, red, reptile ballerina in a hag's clothes.

"Your face is kind," said Allison.

"I am neither kind nor evil," she said. "I am destiny."

"Destiny? That's your name?"

Her smile revealed white, sharp teeth. "No, truth-seer. I see you are naïve as well as gifted." The train began to slow. "You will get off at the next stop. Your destiny does not end on this train, but many of theirs do." She gestured to the passengers, "They have a destiny that does not intertwine with yours."

The train stopped and the voice announced the stop.

"Time to get off."

Compelled, but not wanting to rise, Allison stood. "This isn't my stop."

"It is today," said Etienne. "Worry not, we will see each other again."

Allison wanted to obey Etienne. Of all the true faces she had seen, hers was the most authentic. As Allison disembarked with a few other passengers, she looked back at Etienne but she had vanished. Others boarded the subway train. They all had masks, too. She could see them. Allison waited on the platform, not sure of what to do next. So, she just stood there; and just a few minutes later she heard the smashing of metal, concrete, screams, and death.

Pascal exited the black Mercedes Maybach as the rain began to fall in steady waves. His suit absorbed the rain. It was his duty not to notice. He walked around the back of the car and opened the door, awaiting his passenger. The home was pure opulence, ruling over the neighborhood of lesser mansions and manicured gardens. She was called the Grey Lady by her residents, Philip Rassmueller, his wife Lorelai, and their teen daughter Sarah. Today, he waited for Sarah.

She was pale and thin; a cloud of semi-permanent gloom moved with her even though an umbrella protected her from the weather. Pascal loved Sarah like a daughter even though she was only fifteen years younger than his 31. Sarah's infatuation with Pascal was obvious as she saw him waiting for her. The cloud lifted a little, though not entirely, but enough to allow a smile.

Pascal was rugged, bearded, a native of Brazil. He was also the personal trainer for Lorelai, and occasionally her lover. Philip was too involved with his company and his secret science it pursued. Both Pascal and Lorelai thought Philip knew about their affair but didn't care. He was probably grateful Pascal kept his wife and daughter happy so he could obsess with the other things in his life.

"Good morning, Sarah." Pascal reached for her umbrella, closed it, and shook it free of water.

"Good morning, Pascal."

"To the clinic again today?"

She sighed, "Unfortunately, my father says I need to visit. He is worried about me."

She got in the vehicle. Pascal closed the door and got back behind the wheel. "What's he worried about?"

"Same old thing," said Sarah. "Dumb dreams."

Pascal buckled in and put the car in gear. "There's nothing wrong, Sarah. Everyone dreams. It would be unusual if you didn't dream. Do you know what my father said about dreams?"

"What?"

"Dreams were your brain going safely insane while you slept."

"That's funny, but what does it mean?"

Pascal pulled past the gates and out onto the main road. "He thought that the reason you couldn't fight or run in your dreams was your body protecting itself from getting hurt. And that all the crazy stuff in your dreams was your brain getting rid of things it couldn't sort out or use. I don't really know what he means."

"He doesn't make a lot of sense sometimes." She was staring out the window, the grey day making her own grey eyes stand out even starker. "I'm just tired of the clinic."

"Does he think you won't have to go soon?" He looked in the mirror back at her, "It's been a long time since you have gone."

"The dreams are more frequent."

Pascal furrowed his brow. "If you don't mind me asking, what kind of dreams? What is making him concerned? I have known you since you were a baby, so I am concerned as well."

She smiled at his eyes looking backward. "You're sweet, Pascal." Then her gaze returned to the dreary cityscape. "I keep seeing myself. In different places. I'm doing things I have never done."

"You see yourself?"

"Yes, like I am physically in front of my own eyes. Just doing stuff. Like I'm in a library, and in a class. One dream I keep having is of the Eiffel Tower."

"Those sound normal to me," said Pascal. "Anything else?"

"They gave me a brain scan test at one of my visits," she replied. "You know, the one everyone gets at our age."

Pascal's face was troubled, "We never had that in Brazil. Only your crazy country does this."

"And China. And Russia. And most of India. Canada is still normal, thank god."

"Well, that doesn't make it a good thing," he said. "What is that test for again? Something about the brain?"

"It looks for missing grey matter in a certain part of the brain.

It's supposed to predict if someone will become psychotic or something stupid like that."

"What happens if someone has that?"

"I don't know," replied Sarah.

"Have any of your friends taken it?"

"You know all my friends, Pascal." She smiled, "You're my only friend."

He nodded. "Sometimes, I don't understand your parents. Don't tell them I said that."

"I won't," she reached up and touched his shoulder. "You're the only person I can trust."

"I will always be here for you, Miss Sarah."

They pulled up to the gated parking structure of the Rassmueller Industries complex just outside of Philadelphia, more specifically the "Mainline" where all the rich people lived. The campus sprawled across wooded acreage and contained at least 20 buildings. There was even a private hospital and a power plant to keep the entire complex off the grid.

Pascal had been directed to take Sarah to a different building than usual. It was, in fact, the private hospital. They had typical small talk while they drove, but Pascal's mind was lingering on the test Sarah mentioned. He wasn't stupid, he knew exactly what the test was.

"We're here," he said. Then he pulled up curbside and exited. He opened the door for Sarah, "I will be here when you're done."

"Thank you, Pascal." She looked up at the sky, "It looks like the rain stopped. Maybe the sun will come out."

"Maybe, Miss Sarah."

She walked to the front doors of the sliding hospital doors where her arrival was met by several personnel. Suspicious, he thought. Sarah had never come to this building. He pulled up his phone and checked his schedule. It was clear, and that was also dubious. No pick-up for Sarah. Pascal got in the car and drove off.

Sarah walked inside the vestibule of the hospital. "Good morning."

"Good morning," replied one of the attendants. "It's nice to have you here."

She paused and looked at the woman addressing her. She was thin and pale, with dark hair the texture of a corn broom. "Do I know you?"

"No, but we know you." She pointed to her name tag, "I'm Doctor Smith, one of the doctors that works directly with your father."

"Okay," said Sarah. "I haven't been in this place since I had my appendix taken out."

The comment puzzled Dr. Smith. "I don't remember reading that you had your appendix removed. It's okay, you're just here for a therapy visit."

"We usually do those in another building," said Sarah.

"There's some construction going on over there, so we've moved here for the time being."

"We?" asked Sarah. "Is Bradley here? He's the technician I usually see."

"Bradley isn't here," she said. "This is just routine."

Sarah looked back at the door, "Pascal will be coming back to get me soon."

"Of course," Dr. Smith took her hand, "I will take you to the suite."

Without further conversation, they proceeded down the white antiseptic hallway. At the far end was a set of double doors that had a security lock on it. Sarah was puzzled, there wasn't a security lock on the doors at her regular therapy suite.

She hesitated. "I don't know…I don't like this."

Dr. Smith paused, a bit frustrated. "What's wrong?"

"It doesn't feel right," said Sarah. "This isn't right. None of it."

Dr. Smith squeezed Sarah's hand. "Now, don't give me any trouble. This will be quick, and you can go back home."

"I want to talk to my father." Sarah pulled at the doctor's grip, "You're hurting me. I'm going to tell my father."

Smith let her go. "I'm sorry, I was trying to comfort you."

Just then, the doors opened from the inside and another stranger came out. "There you are, we have been waiting for you."

Smith smiled as she saw her colleague, "We were just coming in."

"No, we weren't," said Sarah. "I want to talk to my father."

"He isn't available right now," said the new man Sarah didn't know.

Sarah looked at his nametag: Dr. Portman. "Who are you? I've never seen you before. Does my father know I'm here?"

Dr. Portman traded glances with Dr. Smith. "Sarah, your father told us to do your therapy here today."

"Why didn't he tell me?" She reached into her purse and took out her phone. "I'll just call him."

Smith reached to take her phone, but Portman stopped her. "Let her call him…" he glared at his colleague, "I'm sure it will be alright."

Sarah called up her contacts and pressed a button. A man answered on the other end. "Hi, daddy. It's me." There was a pause. "I'm at a new different building with people I don't know, daddy." There was a pause then a muffled reply. "Yes, daddy. Thanks You'll be right here?" She hung up the phone. "My father is coming."

Dr. Portman didn't like the sound of that. "Call him back and tell him it isn't necessary, Sarah."

"Can we go back to the entrance and wait? I don't like this hallway." The doctors were both confused and obviously concerned. "You know, all I have to do is ask him to get rid of you and he will."

Dr. Smith demurred. "By all means, we can go to the entrance."

Sarah turned, and calmly walked back down the hallway. Dr. Portman and Dr. Smith accompanied her; however, when they entered the main area there were four guards. Sarah's pulse raced, blood flushed her skin, the pace quickened. She walked to the doors, and they automatically opened. The guards followed her as did the doctors.

At curbside, Pascal was in the Maybach. Sarah smiled.

"Miss Sarah, your father wishes to see you in his office," said Pascal loudly so the staff could hear him.

Pascal opened the door. His eyes locked with Sarah's, conveying a sense of urgency. She needed to just get in the fucking car.

"Hold on," Dr. Portman walked behind Sarah and reached for her hand. "I want to talk to your father."

"Let go of me," demanded Sarah.

Pascal saw this, and with a cobra-quick strike, removed Portman's hand from Sarah's. "You heard the lady. Miss Sarah is my responsibility."

"She's mine, too."

"Not today."

Dr. Portman motioned for the guards to approach. "Sarah is supposed to be here with us. Now. Today."

Pascal's eyes narrowed on Portman's. "Why? I am told everything. Sarah's safety is my priority."

"I assure you she is safe with us."

Pascal looked beyond the doctor, "Then why are there armed guards here?"

"They're for you," he said, "if you choose to interfere."

"Sarah, get in the car," said Pascal. "I'm going to take you to your father."

"Sarah, you need to come with us." Dr. Portman raised his hand and signaled the guards to advance. "I can use force if necessary."

Sarah jumped in the car. She didn't want to be out in the open for what was going to happen. Pascal's fist was like a flash of lightning. The blow broke Portman's windpipe. He fell to the ground, gasping, wheezing, dying.

"You may want to help him," Pascal said to the guards. "You have about three minutes before he's dead." Pascal rushed around to the driver's door, got in, and roared off in the Maybach.

The fragile fairy laugh took the shape of spun glass before falling at Phineas' feet and shattering. He looked around his head and more little giggles turned to glass and shattered. Phineas looked down at his feet, luminescent stones of jewel tone rolled under their own power. He was home.

He could feel the difference in his body as he looked around. He was in the Carbuncle—a rocky outcropping—a travel point of sorts in his Father's world. A soft melody in the form of a snow-flake passed in front of his eyes. They were his Underworld eyes—not that of a human. The entirety of his eye was a dark starfield with no pupils, no iris, just a deep connection to the bloodstream. And on his forehead, a third eye opened that was similarly dark and reflective of a great celestial presence within him.

The prince.

Yes, the prince! I smell him.

Welcome back to the prince.

A small bird with the face of a fox and a bubble gum tongue with green barbs hovered close. "My prince. You have returned to us. We sensed you right off."

Phineas smiled. "I always forget how much I do miss the peace here."

There was more that was different about Phineas, though. He was not a middle-aged man, instead he seemed quite, quite young perhaps no more than 30 human years. His skin was a soft matte grey with white and dark highlights almost like an old photograph. His three eyes were open to his world, and he took it in.

The Carbuncle had held some rough memories for him. Phineas stood and marveled at the high obsidian arches colored with all sorts of fairy lights and voices that would solidify and break. A deep swift river flowed. Across the river were the passages he needed in order to find his father.

"As I live and breathe!"

Phineas looked around for the voice that he knew but couldn't place. Then he saw someone approaching from the distance.

"Surely you can't say you don't remember me?" The man was fat, old, and bald but with an infectious smile and twinkling eyes.

"Mediocrates," said Phineas.

"Your favorite philosopher."

Phineas laughed. "Isn't your claim to fame 'meh, it's good enough'?"

"And it is a viable philosophy to live by. Why stress yourself out with being exceptional? Being exceptional just causes problems for everyone."

"I honestly can't argue with that right now," said Phineas. "I am on my way to see my father."

"An audience with the great Pluto," Mediocrates took Phineas by the arm. "What's going on? Anything special? You turned your back on the Underworld years ago. We thought we would never see you again."

"I had no choice," said Phineas. "I needed to take care of some things—for my mother."

The mention of Phineas' mother quelled all future conversations. If one topic was forbidden it was Phineas' mother.

"I can escort you to the river's edge, but you know I am not privileged to cross," said Mediocrates.

Phineas looked around, "Thank you, but I am looking for Oni." He glanced behind Mediocrates, "I expected to see Oni."

"Oni?" Mediocrates fidgeted. "I haven't seen your oracle in dozens of years."

Suddenly, floating on the air was a lacy piece of spun glass that struggled to keep its shape. It couldn't hold it any longer and it burst into shards of glass. From within, a long thin ribbon of a creature emerged. It was as long as a yard stick and about as wide but had clawed feet near the writhing tail and two more near the bearded pouf of a dragon face.

"Oni!" Excitement filled Phineas. "I have missed you."

"Ugh, do not believe a word this asshole said," Oni pointed at Mediocrates with his barbed, curling tale. "As soon as we all felt the return of the prince, he turned me into a sound choral. I turned to glass instantly but was able to break it."

Phineas looked at Mediocrates, "Seriously, did you do that?"

"Great prince," Mediocrates grinned. "You don't need an oracle that is this thin little fragile waif of a demon that cannot guide you properly."

"I suppose you want to be his oracle?" Oni puffed a dark ring of smoke. "You know that isn't the way it happens."

"Stop," Phineas held up his hands. "I didn't come all this way for this. Mediocrates, go from here. I will come see you before I return to the outside world."

"You aren't staying?" Mediocrates asked. "Your father will be disappointed."

"I will deal with that in due time, now go." Clouds swirled up on Phineas' exposed skin and lightning illuminated the cumulonimbus before dissipating.

Mediocrates respected the display of princely power. "Yes, your highness." And then he walked off into the recesses of the Carbuncle.

For many moments Phineas and Oni stood in silence.

"Oh my god, that guy…" Oni burst.

"I know."

They both laughed.

"You look good," Phineas said to Oni whose three eyes mirrored his own.

"As do you," said Oni, his three eyes looking at Phineas' three eyes. "Why have you come back?"

"I'm making a lot of mistakes and I think I need some advice from my father."

"I told you to not leave. That you would set a lot of things in motion that were unforeseeable."

"You know I had to. And most of this started with you kidnapping my mother all those years ago."

"True, and that turned out to be unforeseeable as well." Oni flitted in the air around Phineas' shoulders, his little wings buzzing like a hummingbird. "In my defense, I was drunk. It's what Oni do. We are sloppy drunks who kidnap young human maidens."

"In this case you tried to sneak her across the river, and she totally outsmarted you and escaped."

"And that is when your father saw her."

"And so began my fucked-up childhood," he laughed.

"I miss you, my prince. Please unbanish me so I may serve you as a full oracle again."

"I can't. It's too dangerous. You would be killed so fast. Remember you are one of the Wire's most wanted, and I can't have that on my conscience so you must stay banished here."

"I understand," said Oni. "I don't like it, but I understand."

"You can walk with me to my father if you want," offered Phineas.

The mention of Pluto and the weight of their complicated history caused pause in Oni. "I think I will wait for you here in the Carbuncle."

"Okay, I will see you soon."

With that, Phineas turned from his long-banished oracle and walked towards the river. A few chorals floated by, laughing like little fairies and then falling to ribbons of glass. He stepped to the river's edge and simply asked the shadows to make a bridge for him. Obliging, fingers of darkness knitted together until a bridge of shadows spanned the dark water. Phineas walked over the bridge, pausing only once to look down. There were faces, people, entire wrecked civilizations at the bottom. Such was the complex fates that were possible in the underworld.

Phineas knew where he was going. He played in these passages and caverns as a child with Oni. Past the river was an entrance to a cavernous throne room—his father's formal throne room. The immense room was filled with trees, a soft breeze, and a large stone pool that resembled one of the Pierian Springs. Ambient lighting gave the space a peaceful spa feeling. Phineas walked inside.

"Hello?"

Phineas went to the edge of the pool and looked at his reflection. It was surreal to see his true underworld face—with the grey skin and three eyes that reflected the stars in the night sky. This was not the face of a man who had confidence—it was barely a man thrust into the deep politics of gods, and he greatly doubted himself.

"Hello, Professor," It was PJ.

He turned to see her. She was pale and wore the dark shrouds of the fates. "PJ."

"Are you surprised to see me again?"

"No, no, no. I am grateful to see you again. We have all been so worried."

"A lot happened to me," she said. "You know that, though. You are the reason most of us are hitting crisis after crisis."

"I know, I am sorry."

"How is Kendall? Is he okay?"

Phineas nodded. "Yes, he is doing well. He is safe. They are all safe."

"And Carmen?"

Phineas hesitated. "It's a mystery. We are looking for her."

"Are you trying to rescue her?"

"I don't know," he said. "Usually, she does not need rescuing. This is different, though. Carmen has let herself become compromised by her anger. I need to find both of them."

"And what about me?" There was an angry edge in her voice. "Not even 'I'm sorry'? 'I didn't mean to put you in danger.' Or 'I didn't mean for you to be attacked and the only way to save you,' save my fucking soul, was to bring me here to your father? How about something like that?"

He sat silently; he deserved it. "I don't know what to say."

"I want to see Kendall. I want to see my parents."

"I don't know if any of that is possible." A stray choral from a fairy turned to glass and fell in front of him.

"I know it's not," said PJ. "I wanted to see what you would

say. I have learned a lot from your father and a few of the others here. The harpies have been awesome to me."

"I am sorry, but I really need to speak with my father. Can we talk when I have finished with him?"

"Ditching me again?"

"No," he sighed. "I will make it up to you, I promise. It will have to wait, though." Phineas turned to the water again, "Father, I need to speak with you."

The waters churned and from beneath, Pluto the god of the underworld, buff and silvery blue, rose. Phineas watched in awe.

"Son, you have returned home."

"I'm afraid it is not for long, father."

"Why? You know this is where you belong. You are still obsessed with the Wire and getting revenge for your mother."

"I still don't know why you haven't wiped them out. They deserve it."

"Perhaps they do. For now, though, I have chosen to wait. There are many things in play, the whole world, the bloodstream, everything."

"Yes, I will always try and stop them. But father, the ancient gods are back again, too. And something is going on with the Earth herself."

Pluto nodded, "A great many things are aligning, that is true. Some may be coincidence, but some is opportunity."

"Father, where is Nemesis?"

"You should do well to not speak that name. She has ruined your life more than once."

"I love her, you know that."

"She is thousands of years older than you. And she has the agenda of the goddess of retribution. There will never be room for you, son. Her nature is literal. Balance. Outcomes. Love is not an outcome a person like her can understand."

"Where is she, father?" said Phineas.

"I don't know," he replied. "The Hammer used all her power of the bloodstream to ensnare and banish Nemesis. She could be anywhere."

"But she didn't kill Nemesis?"

"No, she cannot kill Nemesis. Only trap. Torture."

Phineas sighed and clasped his hands in front of his mouth. "So, Carmen is trapped inside her own pain, and that means that the prison for Nemesis is within Carmen somewhere." He turned to PJ, "You are with the harpies now. Do you see anything?"

PJ sniffed. "Are you asking me for help?"

"Yes, please. I have to fix all that's going wrong."

"I only saw a distant mirage. It was the desert. It was dry. There was a river with a small lake that was almost dried up."

"Anything else? Any people? A face?"

"No, just the mirage."

Phineas turned to his father, "Is there any way we can help PJ see Kendall again? Help her with some closure?"

"Closure?" asked PJ.

Pluto looked at Phineas, then at PJ. "I will see what can happen. But, my dear, you are here with us forever. The harpies and the fates feel your potential. Instead of dying and traveling to peace, we have seen your destiny here in the Underworld."

Tears streamed down PJ's face. "But I want to go to heaven."

"There is no such thing," said Phineas. "It's just the bloodstream. All of it. The bloodstream. And now you have your place in it."

"Thanks to you," she spat. "If you didn't know what you were doing, you should never have ruined all our lives like this. You are a selfish piece of garbage."

Phineas lowered his head, "I thought I was doing what was right."

"Well, you were totally fucking wrong about all of it," said PJ. "I have told you about the mirage. I wish you luck in untangling all of this."

"I don't think it will ever be untangled," he sighed. "I still have to try."

EPISODE THREE

Dose is in the Poison

Deep within the recesses of Oracle Tattoo Poppy and Kendall returned. Kendall's divination with Betty gave them a mission: to find Betty's oracle and unite them. Kendall sat on the ground as the green magic faded back into the earth.

"Damn, that really takes a lot out of you."

"What?"

"That magic travel. Hey, I wanted to ask you: why is your magic different colors sometimes?"

She thought about a smart-ass reply but found it genuine. "I suppose magic comes in flavors and colors. For as long as I can remember, whatever the purpose of the magic determines the color. Remember, it all comes from the bloodstream."

"Yeah, the bloodstream. I'm still trying to wrap my head around that whole concept."

She laughed. "That is what has you confused? Not the baby

planet that is attached to you?"

"I think it's cute. Betty rocks." He sat up, "When I was in my trance or whatever with her, there were colors everywhere."

"I'm not surprised. She is a goddess—probably more powerful than anything before or after."

"You think?"

She held out her hands to help him up, "Yeah, I think."

Kendall stood next to Poppy, "So why are you being so nice to me?"

"You like it better when I call you a dumb motherfucker?" She grinned. "Honestly, you're a sweet genuine guy. I think Betty knows that. And I know that."

"Thanks," he said. "So, how are we supposed to find this mystery oracle? Any clues?"

"It's going to be a challenge, but I don't think you would have that specific divination without some clues of how to find her."

"What do you plan to do? Are you going to use magic to find her? What color will it be?"

"First, I don't believe she is protected by a cloaking rune. Who would be able to do that?" They began to walk through some of the passages. "She is an oracle and should be easy to find. But that means the Wire will be able to find her, too."

"That's scary," said Kendall.

Poppy nodded. "Let's go try a few things and see what we find."

"Should we tell anyone we're back?"

"No, let them wonder."

They continued to walk and talk until arriving at a very inconspicuous suite of rooms somewhere deep within Oracle Tattoo. Kendall noticed the main room had its own illumination coming from stones placed on a table.

"How cool! Is this your place? I always wondered where you kept yourself."

"I like it."

"Those lamps!"

She smiled. "Simple perpetual light enchantment. They never go out and I can raise or lower them as I please."

"Gurl, you patent this, and you will be a billionaire. Totally better than Alexa."

"You're fun," she said. "Come on, this shouldn't take long. I was watching your back when you were engaged with Betty. I saw the divination clearly. I saw a train and an explosion. Or a wreck. Or something."

"The only trains around Detroit are Amtraks."

"Yeah, I thought about that, too. But it looked underground."

"A subway?" he floated the idea. "If that's true she could be anywhere. A lot of cities have subways."

"We are going to try and narrow it down," said Poppy. "And if you want to know, I'm going to use some pink magic."

"Pink magic, what's that? I'm intrigued."

"And a little silver magic."

"Even better," he smiled. "Can I help?"

"Yes, because I am going to use the magic on you."

Kendall's eyes grew large, "You're not gonna hurt me or like do blood-letting?"

"Blood magic is not my thing," she said. "Don't make me start insulting you again."

"Sorry."

"I will explain how this works so pay attention, can you do that, pretty boy?" He nodded. "All magic already exists in the world. It comes from the bloodstream. Different colors have different properties. The first and most important thing to do is called *adjuring* the magic. You have to ask it to come to you. The other word is *conjure*. We will use conjuring and the color silver to call to the magic so we can use it."

"Adjure is asking and conjure is using."

"Good, you got that. The third most important thing is releasing the magic once we have used it and thanking the bloodstream for it." Poppy sighed, "So, let's do this and see what we find."

She sat Kendall on a stool and poured a salt circle around him. Next, Poppy placed four watchtower candles in the four directions: north, east, south, and west—in that specific order. And finally, she took a small vial of anointed oil and rubbed her palms with it.

"What's all that?" asked Kendall.

"You are in a sealed circle of salt within the sacred watchtowers of the four directions." She raised her hands, palms up. "Bloodstream, I adjure your assistance in finding our lost oracle. Please, hear our request."

A thin, bright pink vertical column appeared in the palm of each of Poppy's hands. She watched the lights pulse in her hand, grow, shrink, widen, become slender.

"What's going on?" asked Kendall. "Anything?"

"It takes a minute, it's not GPS." She was irritated.

The light then stabilized and simply stood in her palms like neon pink pencils.

"How about now?"

"You're getting on my last nerve."

"What if you did the silver part? Is that the right color?"

Angrily, Poppy slapped her hands together and the light dissipated. "Nothing. There's nothing to attract."

"Did you do it right?"

"What did you just say to me?"

Kendall grinned sheepishly, "Sorry, I don't know anything. Can I get out of this chair now?"

"I don't care." She sighed. "This is going to be more difficult than I thought. She must be under some protection somewhere."

"I have an idea, but we have to get a cell phone."

"How is that going to help with anything? If I can't locate the oracle with my magic, you aren't going to be able to find her with a fucking phone."

"It doesn't have to be magic," he smiled. "We can google and do old fashioned searching and maybe get a clue. So how can we get a cell phone? We can't use anything here. Professor Fletcher took all our phones and there is no internet or Wi-Fi."

"Sometimes his safety protocols are a bit much," she huffed. "I have an idea. Are you up for an adventure?"

"Always!"

"Good, because we are leaving this place."

Kendall hesitated, "How are we going to do that? We will get caught and get in so much trouble."

"We won't get caught. I come and go as I please."

"Yeah, but you're a witch who can take care of herself."

"And you are an oracle who has some very powerful cloaking runes in your blood. Cleo gave them to you, remember?"

"Oh, yeah."

"Come on," she said and took his hand. "We are out of here."

Poppy and Kendall walked cautiously through the bowels of Oracle Tattoo until they approached the main room. She halted him with a hand just before they crossed the threshold and listened for voices. Satisfied that the room was empty, they hurried out the front door.

The section of town where the tattoo shop was located was old and urban, it held distant memories of more prosperous times. The buildings along the street stooped like tombstones with osteoporosis. Most of the storefronts were abandoned with thick metal bars over the windows. Graffiti tagged them. Every now and then, there was a liquor store or a marijuana dispensary.

Poppy and Kendall kept walking towards the next main road that had legitimate businesses along it—Livernois Avenue. They walked past the strip clubs and payday advance places until they came to a small cell phone store. Poppy put her hand on the door to go in, but Kendall stopped her.

"Wait, how are we going to buy a cell phone?" He looked around nervously. "We are gonna get shot in this neighborhood."

"Stop with that bullshit, snowflake. No one is going to shoot you down here in the city because you are white. I forgot, you're bougie."

"I am not bougie."

She laughed. "You are so bougie, now get out of the way."

He did as he was commanded, and Poppy went in followed by Kendall who looked like a mouse in a room full of cats. The store was empty except for one employee who was behind the counter playing on his phone. He looked up once, but his eyes drifted back down to his phone. Poppy wrinkled her brow as she realized she had been dismissed by the clerk.

"Hey," she said. "My brother needs a phone."

The young man in a red corporate polo didn't even acknowledge he had been spoken to.

She stalked up to the counter with Kendall trailing behind. "I said we need to buy a phone."

He just pointed at the counters that only had one or two phones tethered with thick cables for security. "Pick one of those."

Kendall didn't feel scared or intimidated anymore, he was not happy with the clerk's rudeness. "I'd appreciate it if you weren't so rude to my sister."

He didn't even respond to Kendall and just played on his phone. Poppy angrily narrowed her eyes and they washed deep grey. Around her palms, a grey illumination formed. Kendall saw this and knew this kid was in deep shit.

"Hey, is this all you have?" asked Kendall.

"Yeah, we got looted during the pandemic and don't put them out anymore."

"How are we supposed to know which ones we can pick from?" The clerk was silent. "I am talking to you, fuck head!"

This got the clerk's attention. "Oh, you gonna pull some attitude?"

"Looks like you're pulling the attitude."

"Give me your phone," said Poppy in an even, sonorous tone. The grey magic pulsed. "You want me to have it."

Without hesitation he handed it to her. "Do you want my phone?"

Kendall stopped him from giving it to her. "Sister, we don't want his phone." He caught on that Poppy was casting a spell of some sort that was bending the kid's will to hers. "We need a new phone that is activated just for us."

"You want to give me a brand-new iPhone that you have in the back," said Poppy. "With all the bells and whistles."

Obediently, the clerk put his phone on the counter, took his keys, and went to the back room. Kendall was nervous and paced a little. Then on the far wall, he noticed a TV was playing CNN. He looked at it curiously. There was a story running that displayed what looked like a train wreck. He went over to get a better look. He reached up to the sound button on the side and held it and the reporter's voice could be heard:

The investigation into this massive subway derailment in Philadelphia continues by the NTSB and SEPTA. So far investigators are at a loss to explain the wreck that killed 13 people and injured more than 50 as the train approached the Snyder stop in south Philadelphia. Investigators declined to comment if there was debris on the tracks or if it was a coordinated attack on America's public transportation system. More later as this story develops.

"Poppy, we're going to Philadelphia," said Kendall as he pointed to the screen.

She came over and looked up at the TV, "What are you talking about?"

"There. In Philadelphia. There was a subway crash a few days ago. That has to be it."

She nodded, "Okay, let's do it."

Just then, the clerk returned with the brand-new iPhone. "Here is your phone."

Poppy focused her powers of influence on the young man once again, "Can you activate it and pay one year?"

He smiled, "Let me set this up for you and I'd like to give you 1-year free service."

"Thank you so much," she smiled.

Kendall pulled her aside once again. "How are we going to get there? Are we going to use magic?"

"No, we're going on a road trip."

"We don't have a car."

"You got a free phone," said Poppy. "You think it's going to be hard to get a car?"

"I suppose not."

The sultry air of midday strangled even the heartiest of creatures. Concrete sidewalks and asphalt streets amplified the punishing sun, and the wind was too lazy to blow. The whole South Philly neighborhood was all cement and old rowhouses that only amplified the heat. The car wash had been on the corner of 14th and Traynor forever it seemed. In fact, no one could remember it not being there. It was a unique car wash: by human hands only and nestled on the ground floor of old brick five story cleaning brush factory. Most of the factories were gone, turned into expensive condos in the race to gentrify South Philly. The car wash usually went completely unnoticed, until today.

The Maybach pulled into the entry lane. Faded signs gave drivers options of a hot wax finish or undercarriage wash. Vacuuming and detailing were only a few extra dollars for any wash. Pascal sat in the lane, waiting. There were no workers in sight. He beeped the horn twice and waited another few minutes.

"Don't worry," he looked in the rearview mirror at Sarah.

She was shaking. Her tear-stained face looked several years older than just a few hours ago. All she could do was nod; Pascal was the only person she trusted completely.

He got out of the car and surveilled the bay. Water dripped from pipes, and the automatic track on the floor was rusted. Pascal wasn't there for a car wash, though. From inside the forest of tall rotating scrub brushes and undulating rubber strips stepped three young black women.

"Pascal," said to one who was the leader. She stepped forward, "Always so handsome."

"Thank you, Janelle."

The girl to the left of Janelle, who wore Daisy Dukes and a Pink! t-shirt knotted so her lean stomach showed, also stepped up. "Why you here?"

"There's a lot of shit going down out in the real world," said Pascal. He gestured to the car, "I need you to watch someone for me for a while."

The third girl who had multicolored braids down to her ass looked past him at the car, "…a while? What's that mean? Who is that?"

"That's my charge, my responsibility, Sarah." He sighed, "I think she failed her brain scan and was about to be put down. By her father."

"Put down?" Janelle walked up to the car and opened Sarah's door. "You don't look like an animal. It's okay, you're safe here honey."

Sarah looked up at Pascal.

"It's okay, they won't hurt you."

"On the contrary, we'll show you a good time!" said the one with multi-colored braids. "I'm Tiffany."

"I'm Roxette," said the one in cut-offs.

"I'm Janelle," she offered her hand to Sarah. "These are my siblings."

Sarah took Janelle's hand and accepted the assistance. "I am so confused."

"I bet you are," Janelle sized her up. "You look you saw a ghost or something."

"You're not far off," said Sarah.

Pascal took her face in his strong hands. "Are you okay?"

"I'm not sure. My head is swimming. I'm confused."

"It's the stress," commented Pascal.

Janelle looked into Sarah's eyes. "Hmmm…maybe. We'll let

you know."

"Let him know?" Sarah panicked. "You're leaving? You can't go and leave me here."

"This is the safest place in the city, probably in the country, for you." He gestured to the old car wash, "This is not what it seems. The sisters will take care of you until I come back."

"Where are you going?"

"I need to get some answers, and I fear I may have burned a lot of bridges by breaking that doctor's windpipe."

"You broke his windpipe?" repeated Janelle.

"It was a lucky punch," replied Pascal.

"Yeah, sure it was," laughed Roxette. "We know you too well."

He turned back to Sarah. "Listen, you need to be brave and stay hidden for a while. I have some things to do, but I will be back for you."

"What about my father? My mother?"

He sighed, "We'll see about them. I have to figure out where their heads are on this."

"Pascal, just shut up." Janelle put her arm around Sarah, "You are getting her upset for nothing. Now go, we have her."

"Okay," he went to the Maybach and opened the door. "I have to take care of this car first."

"Take it over to Jimmy, he'll want it."

"That's exactly where I was going to go." With that, he jumped in and reversed the car. Then they watched as he took off.

"He is something, that man," said Janelle. "Now Sarah, are you hungry?"

The girl shook her head. "No, I'm just a little tired. My head feels super foggy."

"I'm gonna take her to the grotto," said Janelle. "Watch for cars and call me if you get busy."

Without further words, Janelle took Sarah by the hand, and they walked into the car wash itself. Water leaked from old pipes, and the smell of industrial soap and car wax gagged Sarah's senses. They passed by two large towers consisting of orange strips of cleaning cloths. Then, there were similar rows of towers with brushes. To one side of the car tunnel with the towers and dripping water, there was an inconspicuous metal door in the old red brick wall.

Janelle gave it a push, "Right through here."

They passed beyond the door and emerged in a grotto of soothing trees. The forest stretched high, the canopy thick. A coolness came down from above, and the soft chirping of birds echoed all around them. Sarah was astounded.

"Where is this place?" she asked.

"It's not in an old car wash, my love." Janelle led her through the peaceful forest. "You can believe your eyes."

Soon, they came to a wide circle of stone benches surrounding a calm pool. Pastel butterflies of yellow and pink flirted with exotic blossoming flowers along the water's edge. Sarah took a deep breath and held it, then let it dribble from her nose. The exhalation was visible, though, an inky dark mist.

"What's wrong with my lungs?" Sarah started to panic.

"No worries, that is just stress leaving your body. The grotto cleanses everyone who breathes her air."

Sarah took another breath. This time there was less cloudiness. "How cool."

"Come let's sit by the water," said Janelle. "It will also help you." Together they went to one of the stone benches. "I can't tell you how many times I have been out of control and these waters have brought me back to sanity."

"You still didn't say where we are," said Sarah.

"That's right, because it doesn't matter right now." She took Sarah's hand, "Come look at your reflection. The water tells the truth, the reflection is pure."

Sarah and Janelle knelt by the pool's placid dark water. Janelle's reflection portrayed a single young woman, confident and ebony beautiful. The surface was glass. Sarah looked in the pool, too. She sat next to Janelle as did her reflection in the water. However, as they stared, a second set of nearly transparent eyes appeared to shimmer next to the eyes in Sarah's reflection. A ghostly second Sarah formed. Then a third, and a fourth.

Janelle's soft expression changed to one of concern, "It seems there are more Sarahs in you than the one."

"It's just the water." Sarah stared, "It's the light. Why do I have four or five and you only have—you?"

"Come away from the pool, my dear."

"You said the pool reflects the truth." Sarah moved her head closer to the water, and all the reflections moved towards her as well. "What's going on? Why are you doing this to me?"

"I'm doing nothing, now come away from the pool." Janelle stood and took Sarah by the arm. "Let's go away from here and talk."

Obediently, Sarah stood. Together, they walked down a path beyond the pool.

Dylan was exhausted. The day was eventful to say the least after he shot Dr. Robert Bain squarely in the forehead sending blood and brain all over his collection of degrees behind his desk. Dylan hadn't been sure he'd even have the balls to do it, or if he would need to. But he'd heard enough stories of friends dear and distant that disappeared right after "the meeting."

It was a fucking miracle they hadn't caught him yet. Dylan ditched his car, stole a bike, and laid low under the highway overpass with the meth heads until it got dark. Every time a police siren pricked his ears, Dylan's pulse pounded. There was no way he would have made it out of "the meeting" and still be the same guy. No doubt, they had looked at his paintings and scoured his posts online. Dylan was a dark man; and now there was a report that identified him as mentally ill, possibly dangerous. He wanted to use his phone, call his mom, check in with Snapchat, but they would be able to find him. He turned it off hours ago, but that was no comfort that they couldn't find him through it.

Dylan had to go away for a while. In the twilight, Dylan inconspicuously walked the side streets to the only sanctuary place he could think of: Mama Cane's. He could go there, slip in the backdoor and into the dressing room as Dylan. Then, Dylan would never come back out again—at least until it was safe. He was a murderer now, and no one would buy the argument it was self-defense.

He made it to the back of the seedy building that was Mama Cane's. In the front was the bar and it was sparsely populated. That would change in a few hours as the first burlesque drag show of the evening began. The metal fire door was propped open with a big rock as usual so the performers could get in without going through the front. Dylan was relieved. He was the only performer in the dressing room. Soon, though, the other girls would come in and he wanted to be in full drag so none of them made the connection to the wanted murderer plastered over the news.

Dylan sat down and turned on his lighted mirror. He just stared. The guy in the mirror just shot someone. No, it was you.

I did it. We did it.

He pulled out a nylon to cover his hair, carefully tucking all the locks beneath. Then, he taped the seam. Time to disappear. Dylan took out his electric razor and cleared off his meager shadow, then took a dry disposable razor to get down to smooth skin. Then, he applied his favorite matte foundation and began to paint himself into oblivion.

"Truly?" There was a voice from behind him.

"Yes, I'm getting ready." He drew on his eyebrows.

It was Tiffany with her multicolor braids standing in the doorway. "There are two cops here. You okay?"

Truly froze. The lights illuminated her face, brightening her blue eyes. Tiffany realized something was terribly wrong with one of her favorite queens. She came in the dressing room, closed the door, and locked it.

"Talk to me," said Tiffany. "I can help you."

Truly turned to face her. "I can't tell you. You'll get in trouble, too." She hesitated and looked into Tiffany's persuasive deep brown eyes. "I had to go to my 'meeting.'"

"…and what happened?"

"I was told I failed the brain scan. My choice was literally to give up my individuality, my art, my whole personality."

"That's terrible. I know something about these meetings. How did you get out without being detained?"

"This is the bad part," said Truly. She returned to her reflection and applied her signature eye shadow pattern and black paper lashes. "I knew I would fail. I already knew it." Angrily, she fired a deep shade of purple onto her eyelids. "So, I used the 3D printer at school and printed the components of a plastic gun. I put it together and took it with me because I knew the metal detectors wouldn't pick up on it." She changed brushes and swirled up another color. "I knew I wouldn't make it out of that meeting alive. I didn't know if the gun would explode in my hand and kill me, or if it would work. Those things are hit and miss, you know."

"I didn't know," said Tiffany. "Then what?"

"He wanted to suck my dick."

"So, you shot him?"

"Yep, in the forehead."

Tiffany sighed. "Well, I guess we know why the police are here."

"No one knows I'm Truly Scrumptious. My family would never understand drag, or that I'm gay."

"Not even in this day and age?"

"Not even, gurl."

Tiffany took out her phone and texted someone. "Well, we have to get you out of here. They're looking for Dylan not Truly."

"Fuck it, I'm done. I'm going to go to prison and they're going to experiment on me. Don't you get it? I totally proved them right about the brain scan. They said it could predict sociopathic or psychopathic behavior—and I did just that."

She applied blush. "You can't deny it."

"All I see is a person who was defending their own life." Tiffany looked at her phone. "My sister is coming to meet us. We can get you out of here and to a safe place."

"Where can I go?" Truly paused and put down her brush and looked at herself in the mirror. "I killed a man. I shot him in the fucking head."

"He was going to do worse than that to you—after sexually assaulting you." There was a knock on the door and Tiffany let in her sister Roxette, mindful to relock it. "Hi, you got here fast."

"I'm like a bird, what can I say." She smiled and looked at Truly Scrumptious. "I love your act, honey. And there are cops wanting to get in here. I told them there were performers changing in here."

"Thanks, but I don't think any of it will matter." said Truly.

"So, what's happening?" asked Roxette. "What is so urgent?"

"We have to get Truly to the car wash. To the grotto. We need to hide her." There was another knock on the locked door, followed by the announcement that it was the police wanting to talk to Tiffany, the manager.

"Why?"

"I shot a man."

Roxette's mouth gaped. "What?"

"It's not like that at all," interrupted Tiffany. "He got what he deserved. We'll cover it all later, but now we have to get out of here."

"How is that going to happen?" asked Truly. "I don't want you two to get mixed up in this. Let me just turn myself in."

"If my sister says you are worth saving, then you are." Roxette smiled, "We have a few tricks up our sleeves." She turned to Tiffany. "Okay, you be Truly, and I'll take the real Truly out the back door."

Truly looked at them like they were crazy. "That makes no sense. I'm…" he looked Tiffany up and down, "…a boy."

"We don't have a lot of time," she said. "Now, don't freak out by what you're about to see. You're not the only one with a secret."

Truly had no time to react. Tiffany's skin began to split from her forehead down the middle of her face. Her nose halved, and her face peeled off like raw chicken. Beneath was an unformed milky ball. As the rest of her body split and shed down to the floor, the emerging form sprouted a new nose. Then new eyes. The form's height increased until it mirrored Truly's. In a pool on the floor, the flesh mixed with Tiffany's clothes. The skin dried quickly and turned to a fine sooty powder.

"What...the...fuck..." Truly stood looking at her own exact duplicate.

Roxette grabbed Truly by the hand, "Come on, let's go before they come around back."

"Meet you back at home," said Tiffany in the visage and voice of Truly Scrumptious.

"But..."

"No time."

Roxette ushered Truly out the same back door in which she'd snuck earlier. They were gone. Tiffany in the guise unlocked the dressing room door, and the two officers came in.

"Whoa!" said one of the officer's as he snatched a glance at Truly's nude body: sumptuous breasts, creamy shoulders, pale flesh, and no pubic hair.

"Put some clothes on, please," said the other officer.

Truly grinned and grabbed a nearby robe from one of the other stations. "You couldn't wait to come in."

"Where is the manager?" The one officer looked around, "She came in here."

"She had something else to do," replied Truly.

The other officer held up a photo of Dylan, "We're looking for this kid. We have information that says he works here as a performer named Truly Scrumptious."

"That's me," said Truly. "And as you can see, I'm no boy."

"You're a drag queen. You sure look like him."

"I'm not. I have real tits."

"Take off your wig, then."

"Real tits and a pussy not enough for you? I'm not doing that," said Truly. "Do you have a warrant? Or are you trying to be perverts and fuck with me." She reached up to the hair on her head and pulled, "It's real. I don't have a wig on. I'm a woman. So, fuck you and go look for your little boy somewhere else. Your information was wrong." Both officers seemed unsure. "If you want to stay, I want someone to record this on their phone and put it on our social media. We'll see how long it takes for the backlash to start."

"No, that won't be necessary. If you see this kid, call us immediately. He's wanted for murder. He's dangerous."

"I don't know that person. He's never been here." Truly went to the door, opened it, and called to other staffers. "Can someone come in here and record this?"

"We're going."

The officers exited the dressing room. Truly followed them to ensure they left without causing anymore commotion. One patron asked if it was a raid, and Truly assured them it wasn't. They weren't staying. In her mind and strange new body, Tiffany knew she wasn't staying either.

Suddenly, she felt a firm hand grab her by the forearm. Truly turned to see who it was, doubling up her fist in case she needed to punch someone. Instead, it was a scared young woman with eyes as large as the moon, staring at her.

"Are you okay?" asked Truly.

"I can see you," she said. "I can see the real you."

Truly pulled her away, but realized the woman was no threat. "What can you see?"

She hesitated, eyes leaking tears and fear. "I…I can't explain it. A bird? Birds?"

And even though the club throbbed with dance music, there was deafening silence between them. She studied the woman: eyes widened by sleep deprivation; eyes glazed by too many images; eyes desperate to escape her skull.

"What else can you see?"

"I see everything. The truth." She trembled, "I am so confused."

"Do you need help?" Asked Truly.

"Please, make me stop seeing the truth. I can't stop seeing the truth."

Truly took her by the hands, "What is your name?"

"Allison."

"Why are you here? In this bar?"

"I don't know, I just kept seeing a path among all the masks. I knew I had to find a quiet place. I need a quiet place."

"You said masks, what masks?"

"The ones people wear. All of them. Except children. Children don't have them. But you don't have a mask. I see a beautiful white bird."

Truly studied Allison's face, looking for her own signs. Was this woman crazy? Was she telling the truth? Was anyone?

"Come with me," Truly took Allison by the hand. "I know where you can get help."

Then they left the bar.

Dolce sat by Calliope's bedside. She was summoned by Nolanne as instructed if the girl awakened, but she was still asleep when she arrived. They were not alone, however; the three black birds arrived as well and made a roost in the corner of the room, scaring off everyone, except Dolce. To this cult of the Ancient One, crows were omens of death and there were three of them serving this young girl.

Dolce was patient, she'd been sitting and waiting for several hours. She dismissed Nolanne and told them she would take care of the mystery goddess. Was she a goddess? Dolce wondered if she had jumped to the conclusion simply because of the presence of the birds and their subsequent divination. Only the girl would be able to confirm or dismiss the idea.

In the corner, the birds began to fidget. They were restless and nipped at each other like siblings. Were they getting ready to reveal another divination? Dolce watched them for a moment, but they did not get aggressive with each other.

"Where am I?"

While Dolce was observing the oracles, the girl had opened her eyes. "Hi there. It's okay, I'm here. My name is Dolce."

Calliope tried to sit up so she could see better. "Who are you? Where am I?"

Along her nail tips, tiny glowing beads formed. Dolce noticed and instantly sensed danger. She had to calm the girl down.

"You were in an accident, some kind of fire or something." Dolce noticed the sizzling balls of light diminished. "You were brought here by the Ancient One. We are here to nurse you back to health."

"The Ancient One?" She was confused. "I don't remember anything."

"Don't worry about it now, just get some rest. You have been through a lot."

"Who are you? What did you say your name was?"

"I am Dolce." She gestured to the birds in the corner, "They arrived and have been keeping an eye on you."

Calliope saw her oracles and felt some comfort, "That's good. At least I didn't hallucinate them."

"Do you remember anything? What is your name?"

"I'm Calliope," she answered. "Other than that, everything is really fuzzy. Where am I?"

"You are technically in Scotland, the very northern islands. You were in an accident or something from what I can surmise." Dolce got up and went to her bedside. Her smile was soft and comforting, "you have some burns and bruises. Do you know how you got burned?"

Calliope looked away, "No, I don't remember."

"Does it have anything to do with those little magic orbs that were on your fingertips a minute ago?"

Calliope put her hands under the blanket, "I don't know."

Dolce sighed and nodded. "Okay, maybe you will want to talk soon. But I am pretty smart about things. I see you have these three great crows. You know, they came to me at the water's edge. And I watched two of them tear the other apart."

"You did?"

"Yes, and do you know what I saw in the entrails? I saw you— waking up. I know these birds are your oracle and that makes you a god. So, what kind of god are you?"

"I am not anything," she said with tears streaming down her face. "I hurt people. That's what I do. Whether they deserve it or not, I can't be around other people."

"I see," said Dolce. "I will tell you my secret to show you I mean you know harm. In fact, I want to help you. Can you sit up to see something?"

Calliope nodded and scooted to an upright position.

"Now, look down at my legs."

As instructed, Calliope leaned over the bedside and marveled as she saw the woman had a flared and gorgeous fish tail. The scales were iridescent, perfectly spaced and layered like a painter had created them. Then, miraculously, the scales rustled and ruffled as they became human legs once again.

"I'm not a mermaid, if that is what you were thinking," she smiled. "I am a selkie. I am a creature most humans think is a myth. My kind and I have lived in these waters for thousands and thousands of years, usually harmoniously with whatever chooses to live here as well. I have seen pre-historic men worship me, and I have driven Vikings mad with my songs until they have wrecked their longboats against the rocks and died."

"Are you a god?"

"No, I am not. There are a lot of creatures that live on the earth that are beyond the small minds of men. Men are arrogant and blind; they think they are the only ones who live here. They refuse to see the rest of nature's wonderful beings."

"And when they do see they want to kill us, right?"

"Sadly, that is often true as well."

"Can I ask you why you're here? What is this place?"

"This is a village of those who worship the Ancient Ones. Do you know who the Ancient Ones are?"

"Just the one. A big giant squid who wants to marry me."

"These are the people who are to nurse you back to health and prepare you for that marriage."

Calliope was silent.

"I get the feeling you aren't sure about that."

She laughed. "Aren't sure about marrying a giant monster? I am totally not sure about that. He said he wants me to be his queen and I can rule over men."

"Did you ask yourself why he needs you to be his queen?"

Calliope sized her up, "And what is your role in all this? Are you part of his followers?"

"I am not part of his cult, but I understand the Ancient Ones. We have shared these waters for what seems like forever. And this is the first time I can remember that he desired a human bride. His followers come and go just like the inhabitants of these islands."

"You are confusing me," said Calliope.

Dolce became stoic and serious. "He wants to use you. I don't agree with it at all. I put the pieces together. He needs a human for humans to follow. You are beautiful and powerful. They will follow you to the end of the earth much more quickly than an ancient sea creature. Terror only goes so far."

Calliope laughed, "And here I thought it was love at first sight."

Dolce laughed as well, "I'm afraid not. There are things in motion that I am just starting to read. The fish, the birds, the very water itself: all of them are telling a cryptic story of dark days to come. I don't think you want to be a part of it."

"I don't," she replied.

"Then don't be. We don't have much time, so we must plan quickly."

EPIS⊕DE FOUR

The Day the Earth Stood Still

The crowds began to gather in Washington D.C. since before dawn. Protesters by the thousands carrying confederate flags, men and women preparing to march in their jackboots and swastikas, indoctrinated children in t-shirts with hateful sayings, bullhorns spouting hate. The gathering had been planned for weeks on the dark web, Facebook, and numerous online platforms. It was bright and sunny, low humidity, and no chance of rain.

Outside the main protest area, police had erected barricades to protect the protesters, and keep the counter-protesters separated from them. The counter-protesters were equal, if not larger, in population. Their signs and t-shirts promoted Black Lives Matter, LGBTQ+ rights, anti-violence, anti-Nazism, anti-hate. The groups were already shouting with megaphones at each other, threats of violence, curses of destruction, and eternal damnation by God. News crews fed on the frenzy like hungry sharks in blood-chummed water.

But several blocks away from the tense crowds, a smaller group of angry white people was gathering. The police were aware of them and warned them they were out of the protest area where they should be. They were ignoring the police and walking with open weapons. Most had their faces covered with frightful masks of skulls, the Joker, and other disturbing designs. They were not moving anywhere and seemed to be talking amongst themselves with walkie-talkies and cell phones. Most wore tactical gear and seemed more radical than the protesters gathered in the permitted area. Drones zipped overhead. Helicopters also hovered, keeping close watch on the gathering. Even the news crews were more interested in the militants rather than the larger protest just blocks away.

Then they began to move like a swarm of bees; they had a target. It was an unremarkable house in an adjacent residential neighborhood that still had Pride Month decorations and flags still flying. They started to chant as they walked.

Faggots go to hell!

Faggots go to hell!

Faggots go to hell!

The news crews filmed. Anchorpersons with perfect hair followed like hyenas chasing after a pride of lions on the hunt. The police stayed back, careful not to intervene all the while warning them to return to the lawful protest site. The mob arrived in front of the house and began to throw rocks. Windows smashed while their vile chant filled the neighborhood. They laughed and fanned out onto the porch. They ripped the decorations and flags down, then lit them on fire. Inside, fearful people only stared out the windows of the upstairs rooms. Then, one from the mob pointed up and motioned for their fellows to invade the house and drag them out. The police engaged at that point. With batons and shields, the riot police formed a line and marched on them. The mob fought back with some pointing their weapons at the police.

This is a Christian country!
This is a Christian country!
Faggots go to hell!
Faggots go to hell!

Before bullets could fly, though, a swirl of purple light formed on the porch in front of the advancing mob. At first, it looked like a smoke bomb or some type of diversion to confound the besieging throng. They hesitated, unsure if the police had attacked them. They hesitated, looking at each other for some type of clarification.

It became clear that it was not smoke, but plumes of purple energy creating writhing ribbons around a figure standing within it. Carmen Perez wore a dark hoodie pulled over her eyes. She was not interested in speaking with them at all, either side, she was the Hammer of the universe. Her purpose had been revealed in her dreams of Matamoros.

The energy pushed before her, knocking the stunned mob from the porch stairs. As they fell, they assumed she had attacked them and turned their weapons on her. The news crews filmed. Drones hovered in close for a better look. The police formed a line. They fired on her.

The rain of bullets simply bounced off the curtains of energy that rose in front of her. Then with a simple gesture, Carmen remembered her dream with *La Llorona* and the revenge she took upon the criminals that took her family from her as a child. Purple spikes rocketed from the concrete beneath the mob, impaling them in the air. They were skewered, still alive, disbelieving what had happened. They bled out as the purple energy solidified into black obsidian. Carmen smirked as her garden of helpless attackers died in front of her.

The rest of the crowd shrieked with terror. They ran away from the porch. The police backed away with their shields held between themselves and this unknown terror in front of them. The news crews retreated, but the drones swarmed closer. With a gesture, the ribbons knocked them from the sky. Carmen began to walk towards the main protesters a few blocks away.

Stand Down!

The police blared with their bullhorns.

Do not move further!

They continued to warn her. Word spread from the crowd in front of the house to the rest of the protesters like a California forest fire. They radioed each other, texted, shared phone calls. The protesters assumed they were being attacked by the police or the counter-protesters. In front of Carmen, most people cleared away from her. The police reformed with their shields on either side of her, and issued more warnings. Then the tear-gas cannisters began to fly at her. The universe protected her, disintegrating the cannisters and gas with an unfurling carpet of the purple ribbons. It moved like a wave, knocking the walls of police on their asses.

She continued to walk, to stalk, towards the protesters. The police ordered everyone to evacuate the area immediately. The counter-protesters listened, dropping their signs, and running for cover. The main protest group, however, readied for her. They talked on their phones and walkie-talkies. More drones buzzed close, filming the event live for the world to see. Some of the braver news crews moved closer with their cameras, hoping to get a good shot of this lone terrorist wiping the streets with an unknown new weapon never seen before.

Two police helicopters rose from the White House in the distance and raced towards Carmen. Still, she did not deviate from her path. The protesters began to scatter in fear, but a few drew their military-grade weapons and took a stand. They weren't going to run. No one could make them cower in fear, they had a mandate now. America was theirs to take back and remake as their homeland.

Some of the more organized protesters in militia gear created a U-shaped formation that seemed to welcome Carmen as she continued to walk. Some took shots at Carmen, but the energy seemed to anticipate their attacks and intercepted any bullets fired at her. The helicopters whirred closer; the police issued threats of imminent attack, but it did not deter her.

The protesters closed the circle around her and began to fire their weapons. Showers of artillery crashed into the purple energy that engulfed and protected her. They emptied magazines of bullets upon her, all fruitless in touching her. Then in a flash, a horizontal wave of purple energy blasted outward, hitting the crowd waist high. It kept radiating outward and dissipated. Mysteriously the crowd stopped firing at once and she stood up. The sudden silence was deafening.

Where the ribbon of purple energy had passed through the members of the mob, they simply fell in half. The ribbon cut them clean through, a swift and effortless razor slice. The upper halves of their bodies slid off the lower halves and onto the ground next to them. Wide-eyed and still alert, the sliced protesters watched helplessly as their own bodies fell away from their still-standing legs. The news filmed it. The drones hovered and hummed. The helicopters advanced upon her position, but no humans dared get closer to her. Then, all at once, the ribbons of energy consumed Carmen and she was gone leaving the carnage behind.

Allison watched from a distance as Truly spoke with Tiffany, Roxette, and Janelle. Allison avoided looking directly at any of their faces for she was confused by what she saw. She thought she had become used to seeing a person's true face. She had seen them all as her life continued after the coma. On the train, she saw angels and demons, melted sadness, true joy. But the three women were the most confusing she had ever come across except for the tall red creature that told her to get off the train. Mingling like a mirage with their human faces were graceful white birds. And the other person that she arrived with, that she met briefly in the club, was the most confusing of all. She was a beautiful woman with long black hair and hard stoic features.

Her eyes were dark, searching, knowing. The image mingled just beneath the makeup and wig that mimicked that woman underneath like a watercolor painting over a photograph of the same image.

The group paused briefly and looked back at Allison who self-consciously turned away. Then one of them walked towards her. Janelle seemed to be the leader of the three. Allison fidgeted as she approached.

"It's okay," said Janelle. "Are you hurt?"

Allison shook her head, "No."

"You seem very upset. Do you want to talk to me about it?"

Allison glanced at her face momentarily, but the true image made her look away. "I don't know how to talk about it, honestly. I can't explain anything. I don't know how. Listen, I'm sorry to have bothered you and your friends. I will just go if that's okay."

"They are my sisters," she smiled. "Well, not the one in drag. She is not my sister." She tried to make Allison laugh to diffuse the moment.

It worked. Allison let out a sighing laugh. "I didn't think she was your sister."

"My sisters said you came into our club and were very disoriented."

Allison nodded. "I'm sure it is just part of my brain injury. I was in a coma after an aneurism, and I have had strange visions ever since."

"What kind of visions?"

"It's so hard to explain. I know I'm going crazy."

Janelle looked down and noticed Allison was gripping a manilla envelope that was wrinkled and twisted. "What's in the envelope?"

Allison gripped it close to her. "Nothing, it's nothing. My medical records."

"You are very mysterious," said Janelle. "Are you hungry? When is the last time you had something to eat or drink?"

"I can't remember."

Janelle looked back over at her sisters talking with the drag queen. "I'm sure she hasn't had anything to eat as well. We have another guest here in our grotto. I think a good meal will help all of us. I also think you will be here for a while, for your own safety."

"My safety?"

Janelle nodded, "The world is becoming a very different place, very quickly. And I have a suspicion that all of you have a big part to play in it."

"How do you know?"

"A little bird told me," she gave a little laugh. "Please relax here in the grotto. Breathe deeply. There is magic here that will help feel better."

Janelle decided to leave the topic alone for now. "Okay, you know what I think we need?" She spoke loudly so everyone could hear her. "We need a good meal." She took Allison by the hand and walked over to where her sisters were with Dylan. "Dear sisters, if you will take care of our guests. Help them clean up a bit and relax, I will see to the meal preparation."

"How long do we have?" asked Dylan. "I'm starving and I have had a long fucking day."

Tiffany smiled, "Not long. Let's get you out of that makeup and wig. And you are killing it in those heels."

"Thanks, I just mastered them. Six-inch stilettos. I do a Kylie medley of *'Your Disco Needs You'* and *'Can't Get you Outa My Head'* in this outfit."

"You haven't done that in the club yet," said Tiffany.

"Tonight, was to be my debut—but you know, I shot that predator in the head."

"Werk," was all Tiffany could respond with.

"Roxette, will you attend Allison? And please get our other guest ready, too."

She nodded, "I will see to it."

"There is someone else here, too?" asked Allison. "How big is this place?"

"It's as big as we need it to be when we need it," was Janelle's response.

"That wasn't helpful," commented Dylan.

"But it will make sense the longer you are here," said Tiffany.

"I really appreciate all of this," he said. "But I am on the run. I can't stay here. I can't put you at risk. I don't want you to lose your club—or this remarkable car wash."

"No one is at risk. And soon, your old life will be a distant memory," said Janelle.

"What does that mean?" responded Dylan.

"You saw my sister turn into you—in front of your eyes—and we saved you. Do you think that is the limit of what we can do? This is the grotto of the Pierian Spring, we are ancient and are really not concerned with modern men and their ego-driven police forces."

That answer seemed to satisfy Dylan. "Okay, I guess we should get ready for dinner then."

"Let's," Tiffany smiled and looped her arm in his. "And will you show me how you did your eyebrows?"

He laughed and it felt good, "Absolutely."

Janelle watched as her sisters moved deeper into different parts of the grotto that seemed to expand when they needed it, and contract where they were not active. Janelle then turned her attention to another part of the grotto that contained a natural canopy of grape vines and honeysuckle. Around her, descended a group of about a dozen hummingbirds. They darted playfully around her head, some zipped through her hair, and others hovered in front of her eyes. In the drone of their wings, she could hear them speaking, firing questions: *Who are they? Are they mortals? What do they eat?*

The birds accompanied Janelle as she went into the space. She whispered something to one of the little birds and it zipped off through the grotto. Momentarily, he returned followed by an attendant. She gave instructions to her, the attendant bowed respectfully, and retreated back into another part of the grotto. She returned with a few other attendants bearing trays of fruits, meats, cheeses, vegetables, and two empty pitchers. The attendants watched as a table of stone loosened from the earth and rose in front of them, along with stone benches. They proceeded to set the table for the guests as Janelle took the empty pitchers from them.

She walked in the grotto until it widened enough to allow the Pierian Spring to be seen. Janelle went to it, submerged each hand-blown glass pitcher, and held it up. The clear water sparkled, reflecting the dappled sunlight within the grotto. She took the pitchers to the table and placed one on each end. Crystal water glasses rose from the stone table next to the hand-cast dinnerware and silverware. A linen napkin materialized on the plate of each guest, folded like a swan.

Not long after, Tiffany was the first to return with Dylan. His face was washed, and he wore soft linen clothing provided by the sister. His black hair was pulled back into a ponytail. Then, Roxette returned with Allison and Sarah. There were quiet hellos exchanged, but each guest seemed to still be very guarded. Dylan saw the food and took a seat. He did his best to wait for the rest of them but couldn't help but snatch a piece of artisan bread. Janelle smiled and nodded her approval to go ahead and fill his plate.

"You are only a guest here once," Janelle said. "After that, you are family."

Allison didn't realize how hungry she was until she saw Dylan eating. Sarah joined the table as well, as did the sisters.

"How did you do all this?" asked Sarah.

"Mother Earth always provides, and as the guardians of the Pierian Spring we are extra blessed."

"What is that? The Pierian Spring? Did I say it right?" asked Allison.

"Almost. It is pronounced Peer-ian. Some people say Pie-a-rean, but it is Peer-ian."

"Pierian, got it," said Dylan as he continued to eat.

Everyone else helped themselves to the bounty. Small talk did erupt. Dylan asked the other guests if they were from the Philadelphia area, and both nodded in affirmation. They did not embellish. He grabbed for the water and his glass, but Janelle halted him.

"First, a note about the water in the pitcher. It will taste like whatever you wish it to taste like. I personally wish for mine to taste like sangria."

Sarah picked up her glass, "Can mine taste like Fresca? I love Fresca."

Roxette sat next to her, "That sounds good. Maybe that's what I want mine to taste like, too."

"I will go with filtered, delicious water," said Dylan.

"Everyone, fill your glasses and let's have a toast," said Janelle. She watched as their guests did so. Then they followed her lead as she held up her glass that was red with surplus amounts of sweet fruit. "To safety and peace."

They drank. Dylan tasted the most satisfying ice water he'd ever known. Sarah had a glass of grapefruit-colored sparkling soda that tickled her nose as she went to take a sip.

"What did you want to drink?" Janelle asked of Allison.

Allison held up her glass; it was a golden-hued white wine. "My favorite Riesling. I so need a glass of wine after the last 24 hours."

"Amen, sister." Dylan took a drink of his water. "I think I'd like to hear more about this place. I am only speaking for myself, but your names are Tiffany, Roxette, Janelle? Come on, what is up with that?"

Sarah nodded, "I was thinking about that, too."

"Would you like to know about us, too, Allison?"

"I would, yes." She hesitantly put some food on her plate. "And this is the best stuff ever. I had no idea how hungry I was."

"I guess we all have a story to tell at the table," said Janelle. "I don't mind going first, and I will start with our names. We cannot tell lies here at the table. Our beverages come from the

Spring, and it will not let us bear any false witness."

"Truth serum!" Dylan stood angrily. "You just drugged us?"

"No, you have not been poisoned. The well is the source of the purest water on Earth. It soothes your thoughts, your soul, allows you to release pain and lies and shame. You can be who you really are here in the sacred grotto."

Dylan was getting more agitated. "Bullshit. Lies. You guys are as bad as that fucking test they forced us to take." He pointed at the envelope Allison still held close. "That's what in that envelope, isn't it? Your test results?" She nodded sheepishly. "And you," he pointed at the girl he didn't know, "Are you here because of a test result, too?"

Sarah began to cry, "I don't know…please don't yell at me." She looked at Janelle, "When is Pascal coming back?"

"I don't know," replied Janelle. "He is out trying to find answers. If anyone can, you know it is him."

"Who is this Pascal you are talking about?" asked Dylan. "He sounds like parsley. Who names their kid Pascal?"

"Same kind that names their kid Dylan," snapped Roxette. "Now you should sit down and enjoy the grace that has been extended to you."

Dylan opened his mouth to cause more chaos, but a faint whisper, a hum, filled his left ear. One of the hummingbirds was hovering next to his head, and he could hear an audible voice in the hum of its wings.

You're a rude little bastard.

"Who said that?" asked Dylan.

I did, you punk.

Dylan turned to see the hummingbird only inches from his head. He took a swat at it, but the bird was far too quick. They were on the other side of Dylan's head now. He stood indignantly.

Why don't you sit down, before I make you sit down?

Dylan laughed. "Seriously, a hummingbird is telling me to sit down?"

"I would listen if I were you," said Tiffany. "That's Mico, and I wouldn't push them too far."

"Mico?" he looked around for the bird again, but it was gone. "Its name is Mico?"

"*Their* name is Mico," added Roxette.

Suddenly, Dylan was hit by a blow to the forehead. The force was so great it knocked him back onto the bench. Dylan grabbed his head, pain rocketed through his body. As he lay sprawled out on the bench, the hummingbird returned next to his ear.

In the beat of their wings, Dylan heard the voice again. "Mico Mortem. It's Latin for flash death. Or if you prefer death in a flash."

"Can you hear that?" Dylan recovered and sat up. "Wow, that hurt."

"Don't be disrespectful anymore," hummed Mico. "And listen. You are in a lot of trouble, and the Pierians are the only chance you have right now. So, relax. Drink your water and listen."

"Okay, I surrender," said Dylan. He straightened himself up, took another deep drink of the water, and resumed eating. "Let's hear the story, then."

Janelle spoke: "My true name is Lucina. These are my sisters, Euippe and Polyxo. We had another sister, but she was murdered by the Hammer of the Universe, Carmen Perez."

"It's true," said Roxette. "My real name is Euippe."

"And I am Polyxo," said Tiffany.

"Why did you pick different names? What is this place?" asked Allison.

"Let us answer the second question first," said Janelle. "This is the grotto of the Pierian Spring. The Pierian Spring is an ancient artesian well whose waters give truth and clarity. The Spring is literally a manifestation of the bloodstream of the universe."

"You keep saying …of the universe…the Hammer and now a fountain. What is all that?" asked Dylan. The hummingbird buzzed close to his head, "It was a legit question, Mico. Don't smack me."

"I know the story of the Pierian Spring," said Sarah. "I don't know how, but I know it. You are the Pierians, the guardians. You were exiled to live as birds after challenging the Muses to a singing contest. And you lost."

The sisters all laughed together at the memory.

"You got that right," said Tiffany. "I suppose that's why we picked the names of our favorite singers when the spring emerged here and we began to protect it again."

"Wait," said Allison. "The spring moves?"

"Yes, there are several iterations of the spring in time and space," said Janelle. "It is the same spring, but it can be in one part of time and yet also be in another part of time somewhere else. It is the same one, true Pierian Spring, though."

"The bloodstream of the universe—what's that?" asked Dylan again. "And the Hammer…"

"The Hammer is easier to explain," began Janelle. "The Hammer is the one human chosen by the Universe itself to provide balance, retribution, equalization—protection."

"And the bloodstream is what?" asked Dylan.

But it was Sarah that answered, "I know this one, too. The bloodstream is exactly as it sounds. The bloodstream runs through all of us, anything living, anything material. Anything that is present in the universe receives the blood of the universe."

"Is it God?" asked Allison.

"I don't know the answer to that," said Janelle, "but we are all brothers and sisters, connected and bound by the bloodstream."

"That's heavy," sighed Dylan and took another drink of water. "Is that it?"

"Yes," said Tiffany. "Did you want more?"

"No. I get it." He put his glass down again. "What's bothering me is—why on Earth did you picked those names?" He laughed, "I mean, come on, Tiffany?"

"I like Tiffany," said Tiffany. "She is a great singer!"

Allison smiled, "I was wondering that, too."

"Oh, come on!" Tiffany began to sing: "I think we're alone now. Doesn't seem to be anyone one around."

Dylan laughed and joined, "I think we're alone now. The beating of our hearts is the only sound."

"See," said Tiffany. "She is very good."

He looked at Janelle, "Janelle Monet?"

She just grinned.

"But Roxette was a group," said Sarah. "The lead singer was Marie Fredriksson who passed away from cancer after a 17-year battle."

"I never looked up her name, so I just picked Roxette. She was so good. I love their music."

Dylan was puzzled, though. He scrutinized Sarah. "How do you know all that—about the Spring and the Pierians? You sound like an encyclopedia or something."

"I have read a lot. I don't get out much. I am schooled at home."

"Congrats to whomsoever schooled you. I have a few friends who are home-schooled, and they can't think their way out of a paper bag," remarked Dylan.

"What's your story, then?" asked Allison of Dylan. "You seem to have some strong opinions."

"I do," he replied.

"Why were you dressed like a girl earlier?" asked Sarah innocently.

Dylan bristled, but Tiffany put a calming hand on his. "She is a drag queen. A performer."

"I know what a drag queen is. I have read about that culture. I have never met one. Truthfully, I have not met a lot of people at all in my life. Just the doctors, my parents, and Pascal."

"Is this Pascal going to magically appear?" asked Dylan.

"He cannot come this far into the grotto," said Janelle. "Let's return to your story."

"I shot a pervert psychiatrist in the head with a plastic gun and killed him."

The table got quiet.

"What? He had it coming. I took their fucking test, and I knew I was going to fail it. I just knew. Most of the people I knew who failed that test were artists or musicians, or someone who really had something special and unique."

"And you are unique and special?" asked Roxette sarcastically.

"Yeah, I am," was the unshy reply. "I am a damn good painter. In fact, I had to take that test to get my full ride scholarship to art school. I didn't have a choice. So, then they called me for 'the meeting' and everyone knows when you get called for the meeting it is over for you. So, I went to the 3D lab in the art department at school. I took in instructions from the Internet on how to print a 3D plastic handgun. I printed one and took it with me. I had no plan, but I wasn't going to let them take me away and turn me into an experiment. If I was going to go, I was going to take as many of them with me as possible. Unfortunately for me, there was a good chance the gun would explode in my hand and kill me, or I would only be able to fire one bullet before it failed.

"So, I went, and this doctor told me if I let him give me a blowjob he would see what he could do for me. So, I shot him. Then I escaped and went to work."

"That's when I realized what was happening," said Tiffany. "He came to work at the club. We got him out of there."

"And then I walked in," said Allison.

"Yes, and then you came in," echoed Roxette. "She looked right at me in my face and saw my truth."

Allison averted her eyes, "It is the worst feeling to see people's true faces." She realized she may have offended the Pierian maidens, "Not you guys! I didn't mean to offend anyone."

"It is okay," said Janelle. "We understand having a burden like that."

"So, you see exactly what when you look at people," asked Dylan. "What do you see when you look at me?"

Mico buzzed in Dylan's ear, "an asshole."

"Hush little bird or I will catch you in my hand."

"Ha, I would love to see that," hummed Mico.

"Mico," said Janelle, "perhaps come over to this side of the table for now." The bird obeyed. "Now, please continue."

"When I look at people, adults, I see their true faces. They may look different to the world, but I see who they truly are beneath their face."

"That must be fascinating," said Dylan.

"It isn't, not at all," said Allison. "I have seen people with such deep inner burdens that their faces are melting. Or someone may be just a true selfish, mean person and I see all that ugly."

"Is it everyone?" asked Sarah.

Allison nodded. "Children and animals don't have them. Their true faces are still the real thing."

"Before adults fuck them up," snapped Dylan. "What do you see when you look at me?"

Allison lifted her eyes to consider him. "You look pretty much the same, but you are a woman."

He smiled, "I can agree with that."

"How about me?" asked Sarah.

Allison looked at her carefully. "You don't look that much different than your real face…but…" she scrutinized the teenager, "…I don't know if it is because you are still really young…but there are like six of you. Just out of focus like I'm looking at a 3D poster without 3D glasses."

"What's a 3D poster?" asked Sarah.

"Never mind," said Allison. "Everyone here is fairly the same as their real faces. And that is such a relief to be able to look at you."

"I remember you coming into the club, you seemed really really upset," said Dylan. "What happened?"

"You know that subway crash, the one that has been on the news, I was almost in that." She played with some of the food on her plate, "I was on that train. I had just come from what you called 'the meeting.' I was given 24 hours to get my affairs in order and turn myself in.

"You see, I was normal up until last year. I had a brain aneurism and was in a coma. When I came out of it, I was able to see a person's true face. It was so horrible. My nurses and doctors. Everyone. They said it was because of the brain damage and it was related to the reduction of my gray matter because of the aneurism. But they didn't care—at least the government didn't. They didn't care that I had brain damage in that area of my brain. I failed the test."

"This test," grumbled Janelle. "It is an abomination."

"It seems like they are looking for more than missing grey matter," commented Roxette.

Dylan looked at Sarah, "You seem to know a lot about everything, do you know anything about this test?"

She shook her head, "Nothing. I don't think I have ever read about it."

"We can just stay here and be safe," said Allison.

Janelle sighed, "Unfortunately, that is not a long-term solution. This is sacred ground. Mortals should not be here. We will eventually have to find a solution, but for now you can stay and be protected. There are a lot of mysteries going on. Hopefully, Pascal can find some answers."

"You keep mentioning this Pascal," said Dylan. "Who is he?"

"He is my bodyguard," said Sarah, "and my best friend."

"Your bodyguard?" sniffed Dylan. "How is he going to find any answers."

Janelle smiled, "He is not just a bodyguard, he is very capable and inventive. If there are answers to find, he will find them."

Dylan gave a muffled laugh of disbelief. Mico whirred like a toy from Janelle over to him. There was a humming conversation, and Dylan told them to be quiet.

What will you do if I am not quiet?

"I will show you, you little jerk."

Mico flitted about, giggling through the hum of their wings. Dylan could understand every word, and they were escalating.

You can't catch me! No one has ever caught me! You are way too slow…

The word "slow" hung in the air. The pitch descended from normal to deep baritone and slurred. Around the room, the trees slowed. The people around the table slowed, their movements like molasses in winter. Dylan's eyes flashed. In his mind, he could see the hummingbird. The image flickered from where it was nearly frozen in mid-air, and a second image flickered near Janelle. Dylan's instincts pulled him, dictated his actions. Ignore the bird in front of you. It is the second image on which to focus. That is where Mico will be in seconds. Get to that spot and wait for them.

Dylan got up off the bench. Everyone else was exaggeratingly slow, like a movie emphasizing an action scene where too much is going on. Dylan walked over to where Janelle was and waited as the flickering image of Mico solidified while the one that was over where his seat was began to fade. He put out his hand as Mico materialized and gripped them tightly in his fist. Time resumed.

"Caught you!" exclaimed Dylan.

The dinner guests resumed normal motion. Janelle jumped up, surprised that Dylan was now standing next to her when only a heartbeat before he was sitting by his plate and arguing with the hummingbird.

"How…?" was all she could articulate.

Allison dropped her fork. "How did you do that?"

"Do what?" asked Dylan. "I saw this little asshole buzzing around me and Janelle at the same time, so I got up and caught them." He let the bird go, "See, I told you I would catch you if you kept messing with me."

Mico was shocked. They hovered close to Janelle's ear, humming vibrantly. She was listening intently to the bird.

"No one has ever caught Mico," said Janelle. "In all of the thousands of years, no one has ever caught the greatest hummingbird assassin."

"Hummingbird assassin?" repeated Dylan. "What the hell is that?"

"Mico," began Janelle as she was joined by dozens of hummingbirds coming out of the grotto, "all of the hummingbirds. They are the most lethal assassins. They protect the spring."

"Where were they when the Hammer killed your sister," accused Dylan.

All three sisters were silent and hung their heads.

"They were afraid of the Hammer. She would have killed them all with a thought."

"Bullshit," said Dylan. "I will kill her for you."

The sisters all gasped.

"I caught them," Dylan pointed at Mico hovering. "I can kill this Hammer person, too."

"We need to stop this conversation," said Janelle.

"Why?" confronted Dylan. "You gave us the water to drink so we would speak the truth. I am speaking it and you don't want to hear it."

Janelle started to respond but held her tongue. Mico was humming words into her ear. She nodded.

"I am sorry," she said. "You are right. I did give you the water." She stood and held out her hand to Dylan, "Can you come with me?"

"Where are we going? Are you going to do something to me?"

It was Allison who spoke: "They won't hurt you. It's okay."

"You can see that, too?" asked Dylan.

She nodded, "Yes, I see the truth in all things. They don't want to hurt you. Go with them."

Without further protests, Dylan allowed the three sisters to lead him into the grotto. As they journeyed deeper, the trees changed. Mico was a darting chaperone. Other birds, of all kinds, swirled and followed along as did the butterflies and insects. Dylan looked back and he couldn't see the dining area any longer.

Soon, the Pierian Spring came into view. Dylan's heart thundered like a timpani drum, and he could hear it in his ears like an elephant march. Anxiety danced on his nerves. They arrived at the stone edge of the fountain.

"This is the Pierian Spring," said Janelle. Mico whispered in her ear. "There is a deeper truth in you. The spring will help you discover what connection you have to the bloodstream. My dear Mico has a theory—an interesting theory."

"And what is that?" asked Dylan.

"You are a god."

"A what?" he laughed. "Because I caught them?"

"Perhaps, but it was the way you caught them. You disappeared. Time slowed."

"Time didn't slow, I just knew where they were going to be next. I could see them. So, I got up and just went to where they were going to be and waited."

"To us, you disappeared and reappeared. No human can do that." She knelt, "Step into the waters and you can know the truth."

"Is it deep?" Dylan looked over the edge. "Warm?"

"You will not sink. You will not drown. You will be welcomed into the bosom of the universe."

"Bosom?" He laughed. "Okay, you won me over with bosom. What do I do?"

"Disrobe and simply get in the water."

Dylan stood forth and slipped out of the clothing given to him by Tiffany. He stood tall and thin, a swimmer's build. Then he sat down on the stones and swung his legs over the side. For many moments, Dylan looked at the dark water. It was comforting and calm, the temperature perfect like a warm Caribbean beach. Then he simply slid off the stones and let the water pull him in deep.

There was no need for lungs nor consciousness. The water embraced him, soothing and comforting. All Dylan's stress and concerns shed like ink, a spreading cloud that dissipated and diluted. The cloud began to glow, the nebula he had shed was returning to bathe Dylan. The infusion joined with his blood, filling him. The elephant heart beat calmed, reduced in amplification. He became she.

Dylan's hair spread out, flowing in the current. She floated to the surface on her back. She was not Dylan, that was no longer her truth. She was she, forever past and forever future. The fountain clarified the truth and made it whole.

She found the pool was shallow as she stood. On the edge, the three sisters welcomed her as she walked out of the water. Her hair was waist-length, bone-straight and jet-black. She had breasts and a vagina now, like it was always the truth. They wrapped her in thick white towels.

"How do you feel?" Asked Janelle.

"Honest. Authentic."

Tiffany nodded, "My goddess, that is the truth."

"Tell us, what is your name?"

She thought about it for the moment. Dylan was gone. He had been a great host who made sure she survived to find the fountain. The Pierians blotted her hair, fluffed it, making sure she was comfortable. Mico hovered close.

Welcome, my goddess. I am your oracle.

She looked at the bird. "My oracle?"

Janelle picked up on it, too. "As we suspected, you were a god. You have a gift."

"What is my gift?"

"It appears you can predict the future and then move through time to where you wish to be."

"I will have to practice," she said. "Mico said they were my oracle. What does that mean?"

"All gods have an oracle. An oracle is a person, or creature, that offers you counsel. They have divinations that help a god make decisions."

"Mico is my oracle?"

They hovered closely and hummed with their wings. "I am your oracle, and you are my god. I knew when you caught me you were different. I am satisfied my suspicions were true."

"You two will have a lot of time to get to know one another and discover your abilities," said Janelle. "But you have not told us who you are. Certainly, not that boy who went into the water."

"That was me, but in the past. I treasure him and how tenaciously he protected us. I will never forget him, Dylan. I am not him, though." She paused, "I am Truly. Truly Scrumptious."

Poppy sat in the passenger seat while Kendall drove their late model Nissan Rogue east on I-90 west of Cleveland, just before the Pennsylvania line. The sun was bright and came through the open sunroof. Kendall wanted the Range Rover, but Poppy advised against such a high-profile vehicle for a teenager and little girl.

"What are you thinking about?" he asked while glancing over at Poppy who was just looking out the window.

"I don't know, Betty."

"Why Betty?"

She sat up and looked over at him. "The Earth gives birth, and you don't think that is like the biggest omen or divination, like, ever?"

"I never thought about it like that," he said. "I just like her a lot. Really great vibe."

"I guess that's something," she replied. "I'm getting a little hungry and I have to pee."

"Okay, I can fill up. We're about to go through the mountains and I really don't want to have to stop. The tunnels through the mountains are really cool, though."

"Have you been here before?"

He nodded. "We came on a family vacation to Philadelphia once." He paused, "PJ came with my family. Yeah, that was a good memory."

"I'm sorry we don't know more about that happened to her, but she's not dead. She may have a new role in this world like we all have suddenly gotten."

"Like this woman we have to find for Betty?"

"Yeah, just like that. We have all been 'stepped up' whether we like it or not."

Kendall spotted an exit sign, "Hey look at the next exit. It's a Wawa. I love Wawa."

"What's a Wawa?"

He smiled, "It's totally fun. Like an amped-up 7-11."

"I don't know what that is either," she said.

Kendall signaled and exited. He followed the signs leading him to the Wawa just under the overpass. The large modern building had at least 20 gas pumps and an enormous center structure covered with posters touting the world's best hoagies and coffee. Kendall pulled up to a pump and Poppy jumped out to go ahead. She conveniently "suggested" to the car dealer to give them a thousand dollar signing bonus—in cash.

"I will pay for the gas. Hold on."

She went in the store; it was humming with travelers local and far, all getting drinks and supplies. Then Poppy noticed the back counter where you custom-ordered food on a touch screen. She approached one of the empty kiosks, briefly studied it, and began making selections.

"Hey little lady, you need any help there?" Asked an older grandpa from behind.

"No thanks, this is really easy." She smiled, attempting to be as cordial as possible and not causing a scene. She took the ticket with her number on it, "See, easy peasy."

"Are you here alone?" the old man asked. "Where are your parents?"

Faint green energy pooled in her hand. Suddenly, Kendall grabbed her hand from behind. "What's going on, sis?"

"This old guy was just about to kidnap me," she sneered. "He won't leave me alone."

The old man was shocked and held up his hands. "No, no, no…that's not true. I was concerned she was alone."

"What if she was?" asked Kendall. "Is that a crime? I thought not, sir." Kendall steered her towards the counter, "Come on, let's pay and get going. We don't want to be late."

"You should have let me take care of the old perv," she hissed under her breath.

"He wasn't a danger, just annoying. My grandparents are like that, too."

Poppy put her ticket on the counter for the food. "This and $40 on pump 15."

Kendall was staring at the TV screen over the customer counter. "OMG, look…" He pointed.

Poppy finished paying as she looked up. At first, she didn't know what she was looking at: a news break about a terrorist attack in DC. It was chaos. She couldn't make heads or tails of it until she saw what drew Kendall's attention. Carmen Perez cut over a dozen people clean in half with her bloodstream energy. It looked fake, like a Hollywood movie production with great special effects.

"Jesus, man," whispered Kendall. "What the fuck has happened? What did she do?"

"I don't know, but we need to get out of here." She took her paid ticket and headed back to the food counter to pick it up. "Fill the gas and I will meet you outside."

As Kendall left, Poppy handed her ticket to the attendant who gave her the hoagies. She was about to get a few drinks out of the cooler when she noticed the old man talking to two people in darker clothes with leather cross-body bags. They all looked at her, puzzled. Poppy spun a quick spell of confusion and directed it in their direction. And as they were mesmerized, she left Wawa.

"Come on, let's get the hell out of here." She looked at the door of the store, "That old man was talking to two people who looked like Wire agents."

"How come they didn't recognize you?"

"They were trying but I have my rune cloak from Nash, and you have all sorts of stuff given to you by Cleo. I gave them a confusion spell so it will take about an hour for them to figure out where they are, but I want to be long gone."

"You got it," said Kendall as he started the vehicle. "Mind if I find some news on the radio to find out what the hell is going on?"

"Go for it."

They hurried back on the road to Philadelphia.

In the gloaming of the Underworld, PJ sat. Her mind swam with what she thought were dreams, but also the possibility that they were memories. A past life. Her past life when she was alive and walking the earth. Just a teenager with hopes of a future, instead she was dead and yet not dead at the same time. A tear swelled in her left eye and leaked like a small stream down her face. More tears followed the stream made by the first.

She noticed a large dark mass approach her. It was not a cloud nor was it a shadow, but a space just slightly darker than what surrounded her. Light seemed to go into it, but not come out. Then, out of the apparition stepped the impressive god Pluto. He was a towering physical specimen, instantly intimidating to PJ. But he wasn't threatening at all, only imposing. He held a large ancient-looking willow basket.

"Do you want me to do your laundry?" she asked sarcastically.

"It is refreshing that you have kept your sense of humor," he replied.

"That's the only thing I have left, I suppose."

He put the basket down. "I come in hopes of easing your mind. But first, can you tell me what you remember? What memory is strongest?"

"Recent ones or like in the past?"

"You choose," he said. "The things in this basket may help you."

"Why do I want to remember anything? It only makes me sadder that I am here and not with my family and friends."

"I understand, and you are not the first nor will you be the last who comes to my realm and struggles. But the struggle fades and you find that we do have purpose. That the Underworld is not what humans think it is from superstitions and tales designed to scare you into obedience. I know you have a great affinity for anthropology, my son has told me. He is very fond of you."

"The prince of shadows is fond of me?" she asked with rhetorical facetiousness. "Well, I guess that makes everything okay. So, what's in the basket?"

"They are called chorals. A choral is a fragment of time. Sometimes is it nothing more than a laugh or something audible that is so fragile it breaks upon utterance. Other chorals are larger and more substantial. They can contain glimpses of the past—a memory perhaps."

"Do they break, too?"

"Some do," he said, "but these chorals are different. The chorals in this basket are the frayed edges of the bloodstream. The bloodstream is not smooth, and it does occasionally fray around the edges and a choral gets shed. Usually, they float around until they dissipate or fracture, returning their material to the bloodstream as essence. But some are more resilient. They are collected by the Fate Crafters—much like the Crones in ancient Greek legends who manipulate the strings of fate of the universe. They in fact spin the thread that I am about to give you."

"Why do you want to give me thread?"

He held up a shiny silver needle already threaded. "You cannot sew without thread."

"I can't sew at all. Kendall was the seamstress."

"Do not be concerned with your sewing skills," he gave her the needle. "Concern yourself with making a quilt of these chorals." He slid the basket towards her.

PJ looked down into the willow basket. There were swatches of cloth roughly 7 inches in square. However, as she got a closer look, PJ noticed they were moving with pictures and images. She took one and held it in her hands and just watched it.

She smiled, "I know this memory! It's mine."

"They are all yours," he said. "Now, sew them together into a quilt you may keep. I don't want to deny you any memories; I only want to help you say goodbye and embrace your new reality."

"Will it work?"

"Just start sewing." Then he stepped back into the darker shadow and was gone.

EPIS**O**DE FIVE

Oh, the Places You Will Go

Pascal parked around the block from the Grey Lady. He drove his own Maserati Levante instead of a vehicle owned by his employers, the Rassmuellers. He was sure they were his former employers by now since he broke a doctor's windpipe and practically kidnapped Sarah. He had to protect her. Sarah was more like his daughter than theirs; he had been taking care of her since she was four. And taking care of her mother, Lorelai, since Sarah was seven.

Inconspicuously, Pascal moved through the back service drive behind the pool house. The mansion was enormous with the main house sitting up closer to the tree-lined boulevard. Behind the house, however, was like a luxury European spa. There was a guest house, a pool house for changing and towel service, and a full open gourmet kitchen.

The house was curiously quiet, though. Usually there were

gardeners or groundskeepers out and about, but not today. Pascal knew those schedules for he made them as the head of security. Also, as head of security, he knew where the blind spots were with the security cameras. When he had them installed, he purposely created the blind spots to facilitate his affair with Sarah's mother, but also to help Sarah sneak out when she was a teenager to hang out with her friends.

Sarah never had any friends, unfortunately. He was her only friend. She trusted no one—not even her parents or her home-school teachers. She was in a safe place, though, the safest place on Earth most likely. Hopefully, she was giving some trust to the Pierians.

That was one less thing he had to worry about. Pascal crept towards the main back entrance that led into the immense kitchen. He wondered if the Grey Lady would be the best place to find answers. Surely, there would be more information at the office of Mr. Rassmueller, but that was too risky. He would start here and see what he could discover then he would expand his investigation.

Mr. Rassmueller's office was off the main hallway on the ground floor. He wanted it there so he could come and go as he pleased at all hours without disturbing Sarah or Lorelai. And to visit his own mistresses for which Pascal covered numerous times over the years. Pascal detected movement in the room just beyond the kitchen. There were workers present. He wouldn't be able to stealthily lurk about with the risk of being caught. Even though he was the head of security, no doubt they had been told Pascal was a danger and to call the police immediately. There was only one way to ensure he would not be caught.

Pascal ducked into the enormous pantry that would be a small bedroom in any other normal-sized house. The shelves were stocked with premium foods, and in the back was a walk-in wine refrigerator. Pascal took off his jacket and shoes. Then he pulled down his pants, took off his shirt, undershirt, and socks and tossed them in a dark corner. He was naked in the pantry. Pascal concentrated. His skin shimmered and lost all human flesh tone. It was as if he had become transparent and the shelving behind him shown through without obstruction. He was not invisible, however, as he moved for the door his skin mimicked the background like a chameleon.

Pascal opened the door, he changed to suit the background. Gingerly, he slinked along the wall and out into the hallway. A kitchen worker indeed passed him but was clueless that Pascal was only feet away. He found the office and keyed in the code on the pad. The head of security had all passcodes, but he was unnerved that the code was not yet changed in light of Sarah's kidnapping. He had to stop thinking of it as a kidnapping; he was saving her from an unknown danger.

The lock hummed and clicked. Pascal pushed the door open and slipped inside, then shut it behind himself. He turned the lock so no one could surprise him. He took in the scene with great confusion. The room was empty except for the ornate oak desk and chair. The doors of the credenza were open, and it had been cleared out. The computer and phone were also missing from the desk. It was as if no one had ever sat there.

"That's fucking weird," he whispered to himself. "What is going on?"

There were no clues left in the office. He did a quick check for anything hidden, but whomsoever cleaned it out was thorough. The next stop would be the bedrooms. Perhaps there were clues hidden there, but Pascal's confidence sank. If the office was cleaned out, it only stood to reason that all the rooms had received the same attention. But from who? Rassmueller? Did he sanitize the house? What was he hiding? What did he want to do to Sarah?

Pascal slipped out of the office. He paused to listen and take in his surroundings. Using his years of training as a Teutonic Knight, Pascal prepared himself in the event he was discovered. Discovery, though, was remote because of his special ability to blend in with his environment. It was the reason he left the service because the others were suspicious of him. To allay their anxiety and prove they could trust him, Pascal was allowed to separate from the Knights and return to private life. A few years after, he received a curious offer of employment with the Rassmuellers and the personal care and protection of their only daughter, Sarah.

Once he was satisfied he was alone, Pascal made his way up the stairs. The Rassmuellers had separate bedrooms and he decided to start with Lorelai's first. She wasn't home because it was Thursday, and she had a standing all-day appointment at Elle Day Spa. She wouldn't be home for hours.

However, the whereabouts of her husband made him nervous. Where was he? Pascal assumed he was at his laboratory office, but also wondered what was going on with the police. Surely, he had called them and reported Sarah kidnapped by her own bodyguard. He made it to the top of the stairs and struggled to control the thoughts distracting him. Focus on your training, Pascal urged himself.

Just as he was about to enter Lorelai's room, he heard a noise coming from Sarah's room. If any room was empty in this house, it should be that one. Pascal decided he would begin in Sarah's room. Gently, he pushed open the unlatched door and looked in. The scene within confused him greatly.

"We know you're there," said Sarah, but a much older version of Sarah. "Don't worry, you're not in danger. In fact, we need you."

"What's going on?" he asked still cloaked. "I don't understand."

There was another Sarah there as well, only a year or two older than the Sarah he knew. "Would you like some clothes? I can get you a pair of my father's sweats."

"Yes, please," said Pascal. "Why are there five of you?" He looked at an older version of Sarah in a wheelchair, perhaps in her mid-twenties. "Who are you all?"

One Sarah seemed to be in charge and stood forward. "We're all Sarah."

"I thought Sarah was an only child?"

The one in the wheelchair raised her hand, "I am the original Sarah. I am an only child."

"I don't understand any of this," he confessed.

The Sarah who left returned and threw the sweatpants in his direction. They all watched as an unseen hand snatched them up, put them on, and the chameleon effect faded. Pascal was visible now and all the Sarahs seemed to like his bare muscular chest.

"Tell me what is going on," he said. "Who is the girl I have been raising…protecting…all my life practically."

The confident version of Sarah began: "I suppose I should begin at the beginning—with my father's business interests. As you know he is the CEO of a very powerful medical research company. Our mother and father decided to have a child and the original Sarah was born." She gestured to her sister, "the original carbon-based life form—Sarah."

The disabled Sarah took up the explanation. "I was born with a severe form of muscular dystrophy. My father was obsessed with finding a cure or a treatment for me. But my disease was even beyond all his resources. So, he came up with a different plan, which I didn't know anything about. One of my father's pioneering technologies was 3D printing. He was developing the technology to print food and water in space for the astronauts. If the astronauts had an unlimited fresh food source, they could colonize the moon and Mars.

"So, he took my DNA, and experimented and developed the technology until he printed a new Sarah—one without a disease."

"That's me," said the confident Sarah. "I am Sarah Two." Then in succession they introduced themselves as Sarahs Two through Five. "The Sarah you know is Sarah Six. She is the last of us."

"I still don't understand."

"Our father in his infinite selfishness," she began sarcastically, "printed us all out of carbon chemicals and other organic material. He did print us to help the original Sarah, but she didn't know about us, and we didn't know about her—or each other until recently. It was because of Sarah Six—your Sarah—who woke us all up.

"You see, our father printed us to go out and experience life. Then he would drug us and download all of our memories and put them in the original Sarah. She would have memories of Paris, riding horses, swimming, running in a field, riding roller coasters…"

Another Sarah added to the conversation, "I competed in sports—but only to give my memories away to someone else. I thought I was his daughter. He kept us all separated like at boarding schools."

Sarah Two spoke again: "We were oblivious. But he was never satisfied with us. He also wanted more experiences and memories for Sarah."

"I feel so guilty," said the original Sarah. "I never knew. I would much rather have all of you as sisters than some stupid memories that aren't mine."

"So why did he keep making copies of you all?" asked Pascal.

"Unknown to our father, we were more than just 3D copies —we improved with every iteration. Until Sarah 6. He kept her here while we were all hidden."

"Does she know about any of you?"

"No, she doesn't, and we have decided that's the way it should remain." Sarah 2 continued, "You see, Sarah 6 developed a very unique ability. When she was hooked up for the download of her memories, she began to siphon information from the computers as well. She was absorbing as much as she gave— maybe more. She left her ghost in the machine. And when we would be hooked up for download, she reached us. She downloaded information into us from all of father's computers. We figured out what we are—and much more."

"What do you mean more?"

"Do you remember just a few days ago when father ordered you to take Sarah to a different lab? They were going to lock her away and experiment on her because she failed the test."

"What test?"

"The test that shows a lapse in grey matter. You know what they do to people who fail that test, right?"

"I've heard rumors."

"They are all true," said Sarah Two. "We are grateful you saved her. And please do not tell us where she is. We want no record of that in the event we are compromised. You see, Sarah Six made it possible for us to control all of our father's corporate computers. We know the truth that he and his father, and his father before that, developed the test. They aren't after people who are potential sociopaths or psychopaths—they want to kill those people because they may be gods."

"Gods?" Pascal gasped in disbelief. "I fucking know that storyline. I have to confess that before I came to work here, I was a Teutonic Knight. We have fought the Wire—an organization whose only purpose is to kill gods while they are young in order to control humanity with false gods."

Sarah Two nodded, "Notice we were not surprised when you went chameleon in front of us. We have known about that for a while. We accessed the security cameras and erased you—entering our mother's room."

"Thank you," said Pascal. "What happens now?"

"You have to save Sarah. She's the best of us. She has such an amazing ability to absorb infinite amounts of information as well as distribute it. She needs no hardware or software—just her. She must live."

"She will, I promise. You know, she has said she has had strange dreams, but maybe it was all of you she was feeling."

"I know."

"But what about you? What about your parents?"

"Our parents have died," said Sarah Two. "The technology on their car failed and it ran off into a ravine. We sent drones and there are no survivors. They should be discovered in a few hours. We didn't report it, but it is a well-traveled road. We have taken control of his entire company. We have also used the information given to us by Sarah to ensure we can help you as much as possible." She handed him a credit card. "Here is an unlimited credit line and debit card for cash. It will never be denied."

"Thank you," Pascal took it. "But I'm worried about you—all of you."

"We have been well-equipped to survive. We appreciate you so much. Sarah's memories of you have proven you've been more of a father to her than any of us have ever experienced. We love you for that."

"It was my honor."

"Your car registration and insurance have also been changed and you won't have to worry about the authorities targeting your vehicle."

"What will you do now?"

"We will be your guardian angels from here," said Sarah Two. "Now go, protect our sister."

"The world went south pretty quick, didn't it?" Stated Nash rhetorically as he plugged in a third TV in the main room of *Oracle Tattoo*. The shop had turned from a hip business to a war room.

"That's an understatement," added Fletcher as he watched his friend work.

"I can't believe that was Carmen on the TV," said Ray. "She just went nuts or something."

Cleo watched them from the couch, "Or something. I guess there is no question that she is the Hammer."

"Such a keen observation," said Nash sarcastically. "So, you knew, didn't you?"

"Excuse me?" Cleo sat up. "That's an insult."

"Doesn't sound like you're denying it," he retorted.

"Stop," said Fletcher. "Fighting among ourselves won't help anything, but Cleo if you know something please tell us. I know your loyalty is to Nemesis and she could be in real danger because of Carmen."

"She's a goddess, she is in no danger from Carmen Perez," said Cleo as she sat back on the plush sofa.

"So, you're not worried at all?" asked Ray.

"Oh, come on boy scout…" but she didn't finish the sentence.

Nash turned on the new TV and put on a third news show. "These are only local TV stations, not cable. Still working on getting a signal in without it being traced."

"Can you put one of those cloaking runes on the router?" asked Ray.

"They wouldn't be able to find the box, but I can't be sure they couldn't trace the signal. It's easier than you think to trace a cable feed."

"How would they know it would lead here? How is the Wire in the Internet infrastructure anyway?"

"They aren't. They are outside of it with lots of sophisticated hacking equipment from military and private companies all over the world. They are not a big organization, but they are super-efficient," said Fletcher. "Where are Kendall and Poppy?"

Ray shook his head, "Kendall said nothing to me. And you know Poppy isn't the most forthcoming person."

"True," said Fletcher. "She is powerful so whatever is going on with her I'm sure he is well-protected. I don't like the fact that they may have left here on their own without saying anything. That puts us all in danger."

"She's never been one to respect the request to stay inconspicuous or inside the shop," added Nash. "And if she took Kendall out of here with her…"

"If what?" asked Cleo. "I'd like to see you and her go at it."

"Look, I said stop," said Fletcher. "We don't need in-fighting here when we have Carmen out there. I don't know if you realize it, but we have all been exposed. There is footage of her cutting people in half with her powers." He pointed at the TVs, "Look. Do you think this won't reverberate?"

"We aren't exposed," said Cleo. "No one knows who we are, or where we are."

"She does," said Ray. "And wasn't she the vessel of Nemesis? And Nemesis is missing?"

"Cleo," implored Fletcher, "I know about what happened. I know Nemesis saved PJ and Carmen after we were attacked."

"And how do you know so much?" she asked.

"I went home," he said and that shut her up. "Let's just say I got first-hand reporting from my father."

Cleo turned white; she knew who Fletcher's father was. "I didn't know."

"So let me inform you," he began. "Here is the truth: PJ and Carmen were mortally wounded. The only way to save them was for Nemesis to take them to the only safe place she could think of."

"The Pierian Spring?" she whispered.

"Yes, the Pierian Spring. Where she had to face my father who gave her a choice on who to save. She chose Carmen, and PJ went with my father."

"Oh cool," said Ray. "Who's your dad?"

"Pluto, the god of the Underworld. Remember back in Ibiza when I gave the aperture to Nash? Fuck, never mind." Fletcher gave Ray a look that commanded him to just shut up. "As I was saying, Carmen and Nemesis were separated in the grotto of the spring. Carmen had full control of her powers as the Hammer and banished Nemesis to who knows where. We have to find her." He looked directly at Cleo, "I know you want to find her, too."

"Believe me, I can't feel or see anything." Cleo softened a little, "I do wish to find her, but I am helpless. Wherever she is, she is beyond communicating with her oracle."

Ray cleared his throat and spoke up: "I know you don't want

to hear from me, but you know—like a bloodhound can find someone if you give them a piece of clothing to smell…"

"…I'm not smelling anything if that is what you are suggesting," said Cleo.

"No, I mean if you had something that was hers could it help connect with her?"

Fletcher thought. "That's not a bad idea."

"But who has something that belongs to Nemesis. Do you have her panties or something?" asked Nash.

"Inappropriate," said Fletcher flatly. "No, but I think I have something that came to the museum."

"The khonshu," smiled Nash.

"I will go get it," said Fletcher.

With that said, he stepped into a narrow shadow by the counter and vanished. He returned the same way with the khonshu in his hand.

"Here, Cleo."

She looked upon it fondly, "I know this. I remember making sacrifices to Nemesis with this."

"What is it?" asked Ray.

"A sacred ritual knife belonging to the temple of Nemesis. In ancient times, it was used to make sacrifices to remain in her favor."

Ray gulped, "human sacrifices?"

"Not for a long time," said Cleo. "Nemesis preferred beautiful things like birds. It had to be pure white and innocent. The Goddess of Retribution had no need for tainted human sacrifices." She grew silent and held the khonshu close to her heart and closed her eyes. "I don't feel anything. It would be right there if I could. I wouldn't have to struggle." She put the blade on the coffee table strewn with tattoo magazines. "I don't feel anything."

"Well, it was a good suggestion," said Fletcher. "I suppose we'll have to come up with something else. Time is running out, though. It's only a matter of time before it all unravels. I hope we don't have to take Carmen down ourselves, then we will all be exposed."

Night pushed dusk to the edge of the sky. A silver moon rose among the few shy stars that were revealed as the darkness deepened. The time for the ceremony was the first hour of darkness. They would be coming for her soon. The servants and attendants would walk from the ritual site, placing luminarias along the path for the new queen to find her king. Calliope stood in soft billowy linen on the porch of her dwelling in the village. They were preparing for her big night and only a few remained in the village itself. They all awaited the luminarias. Then, on the pathway, she saw Lady Dolce walking towards her. The lady was her only friend and confidant in the cultish village. She had a large clay pot in her hands.

"Hello, Calliope," she said walking up the porch steps. "Are you prepared for your marriage to the Ancient One."

"No," said Calliope. "I don't want to marry anyone. So, what's in the jar?"

"You are not getting married today," said Lady Dolce. "You are a queen. You are a god—greater than the Ancient One. I have been around for centuries, and I have seen the gods come and go: *earthborne*, *skyborne*, and *starborne*. Even persistent gods. Here in our lands, we sometimes get visited by a Norse god or two. And you are a woman. You are the god we all should be following: the queen of light."

"That has a ring to it," smiled Calliope. "That doesn't answer my question, though. What is in the jar?"

"Mud from the sacred cave of the selkies. It is imbued with our magic. It will protect you from your own light as you cast it tonight. You must cast your light like never before, or you won't be free. This is your only chance."

"You want me to lose control?" Concern came to Calliope's

face, "The last time put me here with burns and injuries. I don't even know what happened to Ray."

"Ray?"

"Yes, the other one who is like me, but he is earthborne."

Lady Dolce thought. "I assumed you were the only one, but I suppose others could be rising. What is he like?"

"He is indestructible."

"Indeed," was all Lady Dolce could say and changed the subject. "This mud will protect you from the power of your light. You won't be burned."

"Like the rest of them will be burned?" Calliope paused, "That's hurting a lot of people. I'm not sure I can do that."

"You are going to marry a monster to spare the feelings of a cult that will kill you for even the slightest transgression against him?"

"Survival, huh?"

"You or them. And I know you are the true queen of the rising ones. You are starborne."

"Funny, Professor Fletcher was sure I was skyborne. Why would he lie?"

"Phineas Fletcher?" smiled Lady Dolce. "I haven't heard that name in many, many years."

"You know him?"

"I know of him mostly. He is the product of one of the greatest romances in history—in any culture."

"How do you mean?"

"His mother was kidnapped by a demon and taken to the Underworld. However, the maiden was rescued by Pluto himself and he fell in love with her. She would only marry Pluto on one condition: that she could spend half the year in the realm of men because she loved her human friends and family. He agreed. And they had a child."

"Professor Fletcher?" The revelation shocked her. "I would never have guessed that in a million years. So, I am starborne?"

"Starbornes are in a class by themselves. They eventually

have no time for earthborne or skybornes—they consider them inferior."

"Starborne?" Calliope raised her palm and let plasma form on her nails. "I like the sound of that. What is the plan?"

"I will cover you in this mud as you stand upon the altar. I will say it is a blessing for a long life with the magic of selkies."

"How does it work?"

"It's magic," smiled Lady Dolce. "The mud also retards fire and heat. It is used on some of the huts you see, but they kind of forgot our old magic when the Ancient One began appearing in the bay centuries ago."

"I wonder why he chose this bay. I encountered him when we went to Sweden."

"He is known to be in those northern waters as well." Lady Dolce looked out past the railing. "The luminarias are coming."

Calliope watched as well. There were hooded figures walking incredibly slow and they were chanting something in low voices. Each ten feet or so, they would kneel and ignite a luminaria along the path for the queen to follow.

"I will stay with you and accompany you as an attendant."

"Thank you," said Calliope.

The attendants with the luminarias advanced more quickly than Calliope and Lady Dolce realized until the path was completely lit. Without words, the attendants gestured to the path and bowed deeply to their new queen. It was a long journey and it led to the far shore where the giant rendering of the Ancient One loomed over the ritualistic altar. Lady Dolce was her escort the entire way.

I will cover you with the mud as you stand at the altar.

When they come to praise you and kneel, wait. The Ancient One will rise in the bay. Wait until he has cleared most of the water, so he has little protection. Then cast your light—light that will free you. Cleanse you. Free you.

Calliope was placed in a standing position behind the stone altar. The time came and Lady Dolce applied the mud. After that, she retreated to the safety of the bay and swam as deeply as she could. She was unsure of what to expect, even if Calliope could do it. If only Calliope realized her life, and possibly all creatures on Earth, was at stake. Time passed slowly. Other fish and creatures that were usually at the top of the bay joined her in the abyss.

Calliope was alone standing at the stone altar, covered in the slick mud. The attendants formed a half-circle around her. The one she knew as Nolanne began to speak in an ancient language she did not understand. However, from the tone and inflections, Calliope assumed it was not good. They all turned towards the water and waited. Many minutes passed. People fidgeted. Calliope dared think that perhaps she had been stood up at the altar. She was okay with that.

The bay grew dark. The waters seemed organized and turned clockwise in the bay. A whirlpool was forming, a maelstrom, with a rising cephalopod head the size of a building rising up. The followers gasped. Most had never seen the Ancient One before. Some fell to their knees, and a few just bolted for the village out of fear. Calliope focused on her power, willing it to energize. Instead of simple balls of plasma on her fingertips, her whole body was beginning to glow brighter and brighter.

The creature continued to emerge from the bay. However, Calliope sensed something was not right. The voice of the Ancient One entered her mind. It was not Cthulhu, though. It was a much younger Ancient One. He had an angular squid-like purple body with long tentacles with kissing suckers along the length of them. He glistened with sea water.

You are not the Ancient One I expected. Who are you?
I am the son of the One: Zoth-Ommog.
I am to marry your father. Who are you to crash our wedding?

You shall marry me. We will usurp my father and rule together.
That was not the plan. I do not agree.
You will agree or I will destroy you.
You will? Okay, give that a try.

Below the water, Lady Dolce sought shelter in the depths. She wondered what was going on but dared not watch for she feared the power of Calliope. Then above, the sky lit up with a brilliant aurora borealis. Greens and blues streamed and grew brighter until it was mid-day above the water. Lady Dolce could feel the waves of heat from above, but the cool water protected her. It was over as soon as it started, like a flash bomb.

Lady Dolce patiently waited until the heat in the water dissipated. She ventured forth on her human legs. As she stepped out of the water, Dolce was shocked at the desolation. Everything was burned like a severe forest fire roared through. The ground was still searing, and she had to step back in the shallows.

At the far end of the burned-out area, she saw Calliope walking confidently towards her. She was unscathed yet covered with dried mud. Each of them smiled. Calliope made it to the edge of the water, and Lady Dolce helped her into the water to wash the mud away.

"What happened?" asked Dolce. "I was in the safety of the deep water."

The mud washed off her skin, "Well, the first thing is: it wasn't Cthulhu. It was his loser son Zoth-Ommog he called himself."

Lady Dolce seemed shocked. "Not the Ancient One?"

"Yeah, he said he would marry me and together we would usurp his father and take over. It was so shady."

"Shady?"

"Shady—it means to be deceptive or mean; to stir up trouble; just nasty. Shade. Haven't you ever heard that?" Calliope was almost clear of the protective mud. "I served him all right. Just like a plate of calamari."

Dolce laughed. "I like those terms. They are very appropriate."

"I know, right?" Calliope stepped from the water. "I am sick of this place. I think I am ready for a change."

EPISODE SIX

You're Getting Warmer...

Kendall and Poppy hit the Philadelphia city limits in the early morning hours before dawn. Even for a city as large as Philly, it was strangely quiet. It was as if the city were asleep. Kendall drove by following the highway signs. Luckily, there weren't many vehicles on the road in the wee hours because the roads resembled a drunk octopus who couldn't control his tentacles.

"You feeling anything? Magic or something?" He glanced at Poppy whose eyes were full pupils.

"Barely," she answered. "There is some high-level magic shit going on."

"Keep trying," Kendall said looking in his mirror and changed lanes. "I am going to get off the highway and start driving some side streets. Maybe we will stumble on it."

Kendall exited and turned on what he thought looked like

a nice, big road. It was called South Street. He drove the alien street cautiously. They passed closed stores and restaurants. A few homeless folks were slumped in some storefronts. He made turn after turn onto one-way streets in the attempt to give Poppy a stronger signal. Eventually, they ended up near the waterfront of the Delaware River and followed it south. The city opened up slightly from the tightly-packed row houses and buildings to larger stores like Ikea and Home Depot.

"Hey, I just got a surge!" She pointed to some abandoned warehouses along the pier. "By that ship." She pointed at an old luxury cruise ship, moored and rusting.

"Wow, that's cool," said Kendall. "I wonder what ship that is? It looks like the Titanic."

"You can find out later," she said. "We are close. Pull over, I have an idea."

Kendall found an alley that was largely blocked by dumpsters and shipping containers. They got out and scoped it out. Nice and quiet, they thought.

"How about now?" asked Kendall.

"Yes, it's stronger. Not much," she said.

Poppy sniffed the air to get her bearings. There was fresh water flowing, and the salty scent of the bay just downriver. The pavement reeked. The dumpster added its own signature scents. Then, she caught it: subtle and floral and quite out of place. Around her left arm, a spiral of yellow magic writhed like a snake. On her right arm, a similar black serpent of energy appeared. Kendall desperately wanted to ask what she was doing, but he knew better. Poppy was in a trance casting some hard magic.

She held her hands up in front of her own opalescent eyes. Threads of yellow magic reached out for threads of black magic. On contact, they formed a black and yellow ball about the size of a quarter that sprouted the wings, body, and antennae of a bumble bee. The threads continued to make bees until a large swarm was over her head.

"How good at you at following bees?" she asked as her eyes

returned to normal and the colors faded.

Kendall stood with his mouth open, disbelieving his own eyes. "You made bees?"

"If you don't close your mouth, one is going to fly in there," she said. "It is combined magic. Just like a painter can mix colors, I can mix my magic for specific reasons. I needed reconnaissance, but inconspicuous. I needed yellow magic for clarity and black magic for power. Bumblebees are black and yellow, and they will swarm for me."

"That's pretty sweet," he smiled. "Look, they're on the move."

"We must be close."

They watched the swarm move in the harsh sodium streetlights. Like liquid, they poured down alley after alley, then down a residential street. One block became ten. Kendall and Poppy nearly lost them a few times where the streetlights were unlit or missing altogether. They picked them up again at the next streetlight, however.

The bees rounded a corner that had an abandoned brick building with a faded sign saying it was some kind of old factory. The swarm focused on an old car wash with the metal door pulled tightly to the ground and covered with graffiti.

"They want to get in there," said Poppy.

"How can we open it?" he asked. "It's metal and it's locked tight."

"Really?" she sighed and rolled her eyes.

He stood back as Poppy grabbed the lock in a glowing black hand and pulled it apart. Kendall was starting to get color magic, and realized she used black for power to destroy the lock. Then, together they pushed the door up. The bees wasted no time streaming into the car wash and swarming on a metal door in the side of the car wash.

Kendall and Poppy ventured within. The only light was from the streetlights out front. Inside, the tall spinning brushes looked like dark knights guarding the place, while others were covered with strips of rubberized cloth scrubbing strips resembled ugly swamp monsters. Poppy ignored the surroundings and found her bees—or where they went. The metal door was standing open, and the bees were gone. A few singular bees drunkenly circled, but they also eventually went through the dark door.

"Wait," she said. "Something is wrong."

Before Kendall could comment, he was down on the ground after a mystery strike. His nose was bleeding. Poppy reacted and purple magic erupted out of her body. It seemed to animate the cloth strips, turning them into a writhing tangle that trapped a dark figure.

"Stop!" yelled Janelle. "I know that magic!"

"God, someone turn on the lights I am bleeding to death," said Kendall, rising to his knees. "Who hit me?"

"No talking out here," said Janelle. "Everyone back inside."

In the shadows, Kendall got to his feet. He held his shirt to his nose as he watched several silhouettes cross back through the doorway. One stayed behind them, herding Kendall and Poppy inside. Then, the door slammed shut.

"Do you want me to put some protections on that door?" asked Poppy.

"No, the grotto of the Pierian Spring doesn't need your magic," said Janelle.

"What's a Piahrrea spring?" asked Kendall.

"Pierian Spring," corrected Poppy. "Now shut the fuck up. This is some serious shit."

As they walked, the space gradually lightened; there were trees, bushes, and butterflies. Poppy's bees found some flowers. They could see their hosts clearly: three black women with formidable weapons wrangled them deeper into the grotto. They arrived at a stone sitting area where they found others.

"Poppy," said Janelle at last. "It has been a long, long time."

"How do you know her?" Kendall asked Poppy, but Roxette replied.

"We all know her," said Roxette.

"Certainly," commented Tiffany.

"Sisters, it's nice to see you again. You are not who I expected at the other end of my magical bees." She looked at the group sitting, equally wondering what the hell was going on. "Hello everyone, this is Kendall and I'm Poppy."

"I thought you said no one could ever find this place?" asked Pascal, who had joined them a few hours ago.

"Poppy is a super powerful witch. She found this place with her magic. We came all the way from Detroit. Do any of you know who Professor Phineas Fletcher is?"

A smile came to Pascal's face, "I know him. We caused a lot of trouble together in the past."

Janelle gave Pascal a slice with her eyes, "I am not surprised."

"Can someone just talk and tell us what is going on?" requested Truly.

"I will," said Poppy, hushing Kendall with an open palm. She was addressing the strangers and Kendall at once. "I have known the guardians of the Pierian Spring for many centuries. I have news for you if you haven't picked up on it yet: Mother Earth has given birth. There is an infant planet. Kendall here is an oracle, a very perceptive oracle, of the new god, Ray. You haven't met him yet. You will, though." She looked at the three women and Pascal sitting on edge, listening to the story. "Which one did you see in your vision, Kendall?"

There was no hesitation, "Her." He pointed at Allison.

She gulped, "Me?"

Poppy resumed her tale: "You are the oracle for the new planet. She is a goddess—perhaps the greatest goddess ever besides our Mother Earth."

"Her name is Betty!" smiled Kendall.

"Betty?" questioned Roxette. Tiffany and Janelle echoed their sister.

"Yes, Betty. It's a great name. She told me herself!" said Kendall.

"That doesn't matter. Pay no attention to him right now, he derails every conversation with idiocy," said Poppy.

"Hey, that hurts my feelings," he protested.

"Be quiet or I'll hurt more than just your feelings," said Poppy and he did. "As I was saying, he had a divination of Allison and we drove from Detroit to bring her back to Betty. We didn't realize you had more guests staying with you. Betty is getting older as we speak. We must get you to her."

"Betty is in Detroit?" asked Allison. "Who would want to be in Detroit?"

"It's not that bad," interjected Kendall. Poppy slapped him with a gaze, "Sorry, shutting up now."

Poppy continued, "We have been in hiding for years, monitoring the rise of the *newbornes*. We try to protect them from the Wire, but we haven't been hugely successful. We were able to protect the *earthborne* Ray, he is indestructible. And a girl named Calliope who has the power of the sun's plasma. She has gone missing after an altercation in Old Livonia, and we will soon go looking for her. But first we had to find Allison and get her to Betty."

Janelle and her sisters looked at each other pensively. "I think these young people here may be a part of the future that is unfolding." She went down the line, "This is Sarah, she has just found out some life-changing information about her family and herself. And this, of course, is Allison. We will see if she is the true oracle for ..." she cleared her throat, "Betty."

"And this is Truly," said Janelle. "She is a goddess."

"It is a pleasure to meet you all," said Kendall. "Like Poppy said, I am the oracle for Ray. She is a cursed witch that's like 500 years old stuck in a kid's body."

"Not quite 500, asshole," said Poppy. "But I am cursed to the body of a child. Hopefully, that will be lifted soon."

"Are you hungry?" asked Tiffany. "That must have been a long drive."

"Yes, I'm starving!" said Kendall. "We only stopped twice for gas and just snacks. Poppy thinks there were Wire agents at one of the Wawas we stopped at. Wawa is right, right?"

"Yes, it's Wawa," confirmed Tiffany. "They have the best

hoagies."

"Yum," smiled Kendall. "Is that what we're having?"

"No. I will get some food for you and Poppy. And something to clean up your bloody face," Tiffany then walked off into the grotto, and out of sight amongst the trees.

"So, you are a god?" Poppy asked Truly. "How did you know?"

"It's a strange tale," she began. "If you are up for it, I can tell you over snacks."

"I'd like that," said Kendall. "What kind of power do you have? Ray is indestructible, and Calliope can blow you apart with these lightning ball thingies."

Truly did not respond and simply looked at Kendall. In the next instant she was standing in front of him and gave him a kiss.

"How's that?" she smiled.

"That was so fucking cool!" He touched his lips where she had kissed him. "How did you do that?"

"I can predict where you will be in the future and go there before you get there," she answered. "I've become really good at it, and my fighting skills have also blossomed I guess we can say. Janelle, Tiffany, and Roxette have been training me."

"Do you have an oracle yet?" asked Kendall.

Just then he noticed the hummingbird flirting around her left ear. Truly was listening as the bird's wings hummed a language only she could hear. Then, they zipped out of sight only to zoom and hover around Kendall's face.

"Mico likes you," said Truly. "They say you are honest."

"I try to be," said Kendall. "So, your name is Mico, sweet bird?"

"They are also one of the more deadly assassins to grace the planet," added Truly. "They are probably more dangerous than me."

"Like a super tiny Black Widow, that is so cool. You seem so nice, though," said Kendall. "You won't hurt me, will you?"

The hummingbird was back in Truly's ear. "Not if you don't

get on our bad side."

"Oh, believe me, I won't!"

Janelle turned to Allison, "What do you see when you look at them?"

"Their faces just the way they are. They are the real thing."

"Can you tell when people aren't telling the truth, too?" smiled Kendall.

"Something like that," she replied. "I see people's true faces. And most of them are pretty scary."

"So, what is this spring?" asked Kendall. "Is it like magic or something?"

"There is plenty of time for that later," said Janelle. "Ah, I see my sister has returned."

"The food is this way," smiled Tiffany. "Follow me." She handed him a damp cloth, "This is for your nose."

The group settled in around the table that was laden with fruits, vegetables, and a variety of meats and nuts. There were also empty glasses at each setting and several pitchers of lemon ice water. Kendall and Poppy didn't realize how hungry they were and made hearty plates for themselves. They poured glasses of water as well. Kendall took a healthy draught of water.

"That's good!" said Kendall. "Is that filtered?"

"It's from the spring," said Janelle.

Poppy put her water down just as she was about to drink. "Sacred water? For brunch?" She pushed it away, "What are you up to?"

"The truth," said Janelle. "You cannot lie, Kendall, since you drank the water. Please tell us the true reason you're here."

He was pissed. "That was a shitty thing to do. I don't lie. I told you the truth. Allison is the oracle for Betty. We were taking her back to Detroit to unite her with Betty."

"Why Detroit?" asked Tiffany.

"Because we can fucking protect her there. Professor Fletcher has a well-fortified outpost there. Just as powerful as any in the world," snapped Poppy. "And the witches can take her to Betty."

"Are you saying we can't protect her?" Truly's voice was icy.

"You maybe, but have you ever been up against the Wire? Have you fought an Ancient One? Have you come face-to-face with the Hammer?" Magic was pooling around Poppy's hands.

"Stop this," said Janelle. "I meant no insult. Usually drinking the water of the spring is seen as a gift."

"You should really tell someone you are giving them truth serum. At least respect consent," said Sarah. "It made me feel weird, too."

"Thank you for speaking up," said Janelle. "It really is the only water we have here. It is the purest—and does inspire purity of thought in whomsoever drinks it."

"Well, it isn't that cool to do that to someone," added Kendall. "No offense. "You should ask before you offer it to someone."

"We will consider your concerns. We don't often offer the water to outsiders," said Janelle, then redirected the conversation. "Is there more to your plan?"

"Yes, we came in an SUV. We will drive back with Allison," said Kendall.

"What about the others? What about Sarah? And Truly?" Pascal sighed. "I will be fine here, but Sarah will need protection."

Kendall looked at Poppy, "I don't know about that. We only know about Allison. She's an oracle."

"This isn't the Wizard of Oz and we're all going to see the wizard," added Poppy. "Even though each of you could probably use a brain. Do you even know what's going on out there? Let me tell you, and you don't need to drug me with truth water. Carmen is the full-on Hammer and she is out of control. She has let her negative emotions take control. She killed dozens in Washington D.C., for fuck's sake. Don't you watch the news?"

"I didn't know that," said Janelle as she looked at her sisters, "She killed our sister."

Poppy was shocked. "I'm sorry to hear that. We don't know how volatile she is. We don't know how, but Nemesis is not in her body. We fear the worst for her."

"She is a goddess, what could harm her?" asked Roxette.

"Imprisonment," replied Poppy.

"So, you wish to take Allison to a safe, protected place?" asked Truly. "You should take all of us. I can help protect Sarah. I will kill her, this Hammer."

"Do you hear yourself," Poppy stood. "God, I need a break from this. Look, we are going to get a few hours of sleep and then we are going to take Allison to Detroit."

"Wait," said Allison. "Were you ever going to ask me if I wanted to go?"

"Do you want to go?" asked Kendall. "Sorry, that I didn't think of that before."

Allison paused and thought about her options. "Yes, I'll go. There's nothing left for me here. I can't ever leave this building because I see the faces—and I failed my test. The authorities would pick me up eventually. So, I will go."

"I want to go, too." Sarah stood. "I want a life. I have lived sheltered in a cage all my life. I want to just disappear and have a life of my own. And if that's in Detroit, so be it."

Pascal went to Sarah, "No, I will protect you. It's my job."

Sarah took his hands in her own, "I know you love me, Pascal. It's not your job anymore. I am ready to grow up and move on. I need to learn to take care of myself."

"Look at these people," said Pascal. "These are gods, warriors, and witches. You were raised by a helicopter mad scientist. You have no magic powers or fighting skills, and that makes me quite afraid if you meet up with Wire agents."

"I will go, too. I will protect her—we will protect her," said Truly. "Like all of you, my life here is nothing. I've murdered a man. I failed my own test. But now I realize I am in my true body, my true identity, and I want more." She turned and faced Kendall, "I think we're all in."

"I have a few things to close out here, but I know where you are going and will meet you there," said Pascal. "I will come to Detroit, too."

"I think there is one thing I need to do, though," said Kendall. "Allison, can I hold your hands for a minute? I know it sounds weird, but I found out that oracles can only be awakened by other oracles. Nemesis' oracle, Cleo, awakened me."

"Will it hurt?" she asked.

Kendall laughed, "No, it doesn't. I can give you a protection rune, too. I have a lot, which Cleo also gave me."

"What do I do?"

"Nothing, just let me hold your hands and I think it will work."

Kendall and Allison got up and moved closer together. She offered her hands to him, and Kendall softly took them in his own. Instantaneously, Allison felt the rush of the bloodstream. Closing her eyes, it was the sweetest high to her. Crazy anxious thoughts were suddenly tame and made sense. Kendall watched as a rune appeared on his wrist and travelled to her forearm where it vanished. Then, he broke the contact.

"How do you feel?" asked Janelle.

"Peaceful," she replied. "I can hear a new voice in my head. It's sweet and kind."

"That's Betty," smiled Kendall. "I totally know that feeling,"

"I can give protection to the rest of you," said Poppy. "It will hide you from the Wire."

"I don't want to hide from them," said Truly. "I'm ready for them to know who I am."

"What do you mean?" asked Janelle.

"I want to do one final show at the bar," she said. "If what you say is true, then they will come for me. It will be my time to shine. They will never forget me and will think twice about attacking us. You have to put your enemy down hard, without mercy, so they can't come back."

"I guess we should all rest up, then. Tonight, you can do your last number, and then we will hit the road from there since we will be exposed."

Truly nodded. "It will be something you will never forget."

Nemesis fussed as she tried to sleep in the twin bed afforded to her. She tossed and pulled at the child's blanket that was too small to cover her feet. The smell of heat and dust finally woke her. She sat up, hoping that her prison was a dream. It was quite real, though.

Her back hurt, and a goddess never had back pain. The bed was nothing but a thin, old pad stuffed with something already worn into lumps. She sat up, turned her body, and stayed on the bed. Ancient springs squeaked and protested her presence. Nemesis had been staring at the same four walls for such a long time, she was unsure about how long she was in there. At first, she began to make tick marks on the wall with a fork. When she got to three, however, she awoke to find the wall covered in hundreds of tick marks. How long had she been a prisoner? It appeared even she lost track.

"Are you hungry?" Carmen stood at the doorway.

"Why are you doing all of this?" asked Nemesis. "You are defiling the power of the bloodstream. This is not how the Hammer is supposed to wield her power."

"And you would know, you were the Hammer before," said Carmen. "I've been in your mind just like you were in mind. That goes both ways. Remember? I was your 'vessel' to return to the mortal world."

"I made the wrong choice, apparently."

"It wasn't you. It was that bastard Phineas Fletcher. I found out how many young women—three—had died before me going through his trials. And what was he looking for? He told me it was to find the Hammer. But it wasn't. He was looking for you."

"I can't tell you what he was doing or planning," said Nemesis. "I do not know. I don't need him to return to the world. I come when the universe compels me to appear. I don't need him to find a vessel for me."

"Well, he thought differently."

"I already chose you as a vessel and when you were selected by the universe to be the Hammer as well—I have never seen anything like that happen before."

"All I know is I am free of you. I am free of him. I have all this power and its mine."

"It isn't yours. The bloodstream will eventually take it from you if you use it against its will."

"And what is the will of the universe?" asked Carmen. "Sounds like you used it for the will of Nemesis."

"I am the Goddess of Retribution; it is my job to judge and deliver appropriate corrections to any place I am called. Yes, I used the power of the Hammer when it was mine, but it was taken from me for doing it. The Hammer lay dormant for centuries until you were called upon to yield it."

"And I will do what you did," she said. "I will use it to clean the world before it is taken from me. Did you know I just killed dozens?"

"What?" Nemesis stood from the bed and went to the door. "You didn't. You don't know what you've started. Did people see you?"

"The world saw me cleanse a whole bunch of white supremacists from the face of this earth. I killed a cancer of hate. Those are the people who've murdered hundreds of my people. Raped how many women? Killed how many innocents?"

"Those people you killed didn't do that," said Nemesis.

"Their ideas did. Their beliefs did. Do you think any one of them wouldn't do it if they could and know they could get away with it?" Carmen's eyes were a deep, impenetrable purple. "That's the reason the Hammer was given to me. I think it is the same reason you came back, too. We are supposed to work together to exterminate the evil. I will kill their ideas when I kill their bodies."

"You can't exterminate ideas," said Nemesis. "You can only work to change them. Killing them will only make more believers out there."

"Why? Because a Latina girl who has been abused by every system out there was given a tool to wipe them out? No, that is what I am supposed to do. That is why the Hammer listens to me."

"Look at how dark you are," said Nemesis. "Your aura, your eyes, your soul—the deeper and opaquer the color gets the harder it will be for you to exercise judgement."

"I am exercising judgement," she responded. "This room you are in. This is the room I lived in for most of my childhood. That is my bed that I shared with my sister. I have already witnessed the murder of my family. I was left here to live on my own. My sister died because of me. It was only the two of us. She got sick, but we were like poison to our town. Everyone was afraid to help us."

"I'm sorry, I didn't know that."

"Of course, you didn't. Do gods really even know what happens to us losers? Normal people? People victimized over and over and over?" Carmen spat. "Save your sympathy. Maybe I should start by killing gods."

"Let me go, I am not your enemy."

"Aren't you? I suppose if I did you would go back to Professor Fletcher and the two of you can hatch a plan to kill me or something."

"I promise, I would not do that. I don't want to kill you. I want to help you."

"What would you do to help me?" asked Carmen. "And why would a god help a mere mortal that has done, and is about to do, some more terrible things to those who deserve it. If you were as powerful as you say you are, why not just bust out of this prison?"

"I don't know what or how you did this, but I can't. You know that. You taunt me about it just to have power over me." Nemesis sighed, "That is not the actions of a brave Hammer, but a desperate, scared Hammer. You think I will kill you. I can, but I won't. You didn't get into the depths of my mind like you think you did. You are receiving bad advice from someone or something."

"I did, you're right. His name was Phineas Fletcher. And I got free of him."

"Is he your next revenge target?" asked Nemesis.

"Eventually," she replied. "Right now, I am learning how to use the powers of the Hammer. There is still some Latina and feminine retribution I must deliver. And it has to be public, so the world knows what it has to deal with."

"This isn't going to go like you hope," warned Nemesis.

Just then, another figure, face draped in black lace, a floral crown of dead flowers, and the mourning garb of a child murderer stood next to Carmen. Beneath the lace, the shadow of a skull bejeweled and painted offered only a suggestion of the evil inside.

"La Llorona." Nemesis recognized her. "It is you influencing this girl. Let her go."

"She isn't going anywhere," said Carmen. "Who do you think saved me after my sister died, my parents were murdered, and my own village shunned me? She did. She fed me and assisted me to the border of the United States. She helped me cross over. She influenced many to get me into the system. I was adopted by a white family—where I was raped and abused until I left on my own. I was on the streets, surviving. I started to make something of myself, but I began to lose my eyesight. La Llorona never left me. Who do you think fed me? Found money for me? Got me into a school? Cast illusions so adults would never catch on?"

Nemesis glared at La Llorona, "She didn't do any of that to help you, Carmen. She is a cursed demon. She has claimed you."

"So what?" Carmen wiped tears from her eyes. "She wanted me. She loved me. She saved me when I should have died."

"That's not love," urged Nemesis. She watched as La Llorona smiled her cracked skull smile and dissipated like mist. "Free me. I will free you from her."

"I don't want to be free from her," said Carmen. "I love her."

Nemesis had no words.

"Let me show you what I have just learned," said Carmen.

As the words left her mouth, she vanished in a deep purple mist. Moments later, Carmen returned to the same spot with something in her hands about the size of a basketball but covered with the lace of La Llorona. She pulled the fabric away, but Nemesis still couldn't recognize what she held. It had hair, it was dark and matted, and she could see two tiny grey horns on the other side facing Carmen.

"What is that?" Nemesis asked.

"Here is some proof that I will do what I say I will do."

Carmen dumped the head over the threshold, and it rolled for a moment before coming to a stop. Nemesis gagged. In front of her, staring with three dead open eyes was the demon form of Phineas. His mouth was slightly agape, his purple tongue protruded just an inch, his eyes were wide—all three of them—and frozen in astonishment.

"I have work to do," said Carmen and then she was gone.

Phineas grabbed his neck as pain seared through it. He coughed and gagged, which cause Nash, Ray, and Cleo to come to his aid. They were confused as he held his hands to his throat, indicating he couldn't breathe. Then as suddenly as the attack happened, it was over.

"What was that?" asked Ray, tapping him on the back with a hand veiled in thin, golden light.

"Did you eat or drink something and choked on it?" asked Cleo.

"We're all standing right here," reminded Nash. "He didn't eat anything."

"I don't know what it was," said Fletcher. "I never felt something like that before. It was like I was drowning. I couldn't breathe. Then there was this horrible feeling like something slicing across my neck."

"I know this is a long shot, but you're a god, right? Because of your dad and all."

"Yes, yes, what are you getting at?"

"Where's your oracle?" asked Ray. "Don't all gods have an oracle? Maybe they know what happened. Maybe that was a divination. Did I say that right?"

Phineas shook his head. "That's a good idea, but it isn't going to be feasible. My oracle is banished to the Underworld."

"Banished to the Underworld?" Cleo was shocked. "How the fuck did that happen?"

"I did it to protect him from the Wire," answered Phineas. "We had gotten on the bad side of the Wire, I was undercover really making a mess of things for them with false leads, and agents who had a lot of accidents. Then they discovered my oracle, and subsequently, my true identity. I had to hide Oni in the safest place possible so I banished him to the Underworld."

"That's a lot of love," said Nash sarcastically.

"It was," snapped Fletcher. "If you only knew Oni. He can be formidable, but he is small and fragile. They'd kill him so easily. I couldn't let that happen. Oni is my best friend. He was my only friend as a child. I kept him hidden from everyone, even you Jesse. I couldn't let anything happen to him. Banishment sealed him to the Underworld. He can't leave no matter what. Only I can release him from it."

"With things going like they're going, maybe you should release him. We can protect him. The more information we can get the better chances we have of finding Carmen and Nemesis. You are connected deeply to them both," said Cleo. "It only makes sense that he may have divinations connected to them."

Fletcher considered her argument. "I don't know. It would be very dangerous."

Ray made a large, glowing, free-floating spherical shield. "I could put him in this. No one can touch him."

"I appreciate that," said Phineas. "But do you even know how long you can sustain a shield that is not connected to your body?"

"I've been practicing. I made a bunch of baseball-sized ones in my room about a week ago. They're still down there. Still strong as ever."

"We need to know what that attack was," said Cleo. "We need to know if someone, or some thing, has its sights on you."

Nash speculated, "Do you think Carmen has it out for you?"

"Why should she?"

"Oh, I don't know," began Nash. "You kind of kidnapped her. Put her through a bunch of horrible training and tests because she was blind, and you thought she may be Nemesis."

"I took care of her and protected her," replied Fletcher defensively. "But you are right, I did have other motives and perhaps I was blinded by them."

"I'd hate you," stated Cleo.

"I kind of would, too," said Ray. "No offense."

The muscle in Fletcher's jaw jumped. "Maybe, you're right."

"Yes, we are," said Cleo. "Go get him."

Fletcher looked around the room to find a shadow. Unsatisfied, he grabbed a goose-neck lamp on the counter and aimed it at the wall. Then, in front of the beam, he put a coffee cup which cast a shadow on the wall. Fletcher walked through the shadow and was once again in the Underworld.

"Oni!" shouted the Prince of Shadows. "Oni!"

In a pop of flame, Oni appeared. "My prince calls me!" He zoomed around, flipping his thin ribbon-like tail in the air, leaving tiny firework explosions. "Are we going to play a game? It's been forever."

"No, I'm not here to play a game with you," said Fletcher. "I came to ask if you had any divinations about me? Any at all?"

Oni was silent. His riotous anticipations sank into dread. "I dare not say."

"I am your god; I command you to tell me."

Oni resisted. "You may not like it…"

"Oni…" Phineas' three eyes flared with the image of the universe swirling. "I command."

"There was a divination," he reluctantly said. "It happened not long ago."

"How long ago?"

"My prince, why are you now interested in divinations? I have had so many over the years and you have never come back to even ask if I have had one."

"What was it?"

Oni sighed, realizing his god was not going to give up. "She cut your head off. In the future. Carmen cut your head off."

Phineas rubbed his neck in remembrance. "That bitch."

"I swear that is all I saw," said Oni.

"Did you tell anyone?"

"No. I would never tell anyone about your divinations. You made that clear."

"They are just guesses at what they mean," he said aloud trying to convince himself. "The chances of it coming to pass are scattershot."

"Then why do you still go by divinations for the others?"

"What others?" Phineas asked.

"I may be banished, but I am connected to you. You know that," said Oni. "And I love you. I care about you."

"I care about you, too." Phineas sighed. "It's like everything is closing in. Falling apart. I can't stop it. And I can't see it coming."

"I know that makes you anxious," said Oni. "I know you can't predict or stop what's happened—or will happen."

"I'm worried that I put so many people in danger," he said.

"You gave them a fighting chance. Do you think Ray or Calliope would be alive now if you hadn't protected them? The whole of the world owes you a thanks."

"Except Carmen," said Phineas. "I was totally selfish. And the three others."

"They are down here, your father has taken care of them. They do not suffer and are in bliss."

"And PJ? She's my fault, too."

"She has found a higher purpose, too," said Oni.

"Oh?" asked Phineas. "What has been going on down here that I don't know about?"

"Forgive me, my prince. You have not had much interest of what goes on down here for quite a long time. And now you are interested?"

"I know, I know," he sighed. "I have really fucked up a lot of things." He looked at Oni, "I need you. I need you with me. I'm so scared, though, that you will be in danger."

"I will be fine, sire. Let me serve by your side again. Like the old days."

"You and I remember the past very differently," said Phineas. "But I need you. I need your divinations to understand things like what just happened with Carmen. To me, that means she is mastering temporal travel in the bloodstream. That is very dangerous."

"So, I am not banished anymore?"

"You are not banished anymore," relented Phineas. "Let's return to the tattoo shop, but there are rules or I will banish you in a heartbeat. First, you must obey all my words. You are not allowed to take chances or do things on your own. You must stay close so you can be protected."

"Will you give me a protection rune?"

"We will figure something out, I promise." He let Oni wrapped gently around his neck.

The Prince of Shadows and his oracle picked a random shadow of many in the Underworld. They passed effortlessly between realms and reappeared only ten seconds after Phineas had left them.

"Hey!" shouted Ray, "You just left."

"Time is different on that side," said Fletcher.

"Cool scarf," commented Ray. "What did your oracle have to say?"

Oni unfurled his body. He flared the red fiery mane around his dragon face, and took some laps around the ceiling of the shop.

"I had a lot to say!" Oni floated to a stop along his god's side.

Cleo grinned, "This is your oracle? How cool. I have never

seen an Oni in real life."

"What's an Oni?" asked Ray.

"A very, very cool Japanese troublemaker," she answered.

Oni bowed, "I have given up that life to be the oracle of the Prince of Shadows."

"Prince of Shadows, huh?" smirked Nash.

"Don't act like you didn't know that," stated Fletcher. He changed the subject, "It appears there was a divination. Oni saw Carmen travel to the future and cut my head off."

"Oh, my God!" exclaimed Cleo. "That's horrible!"

"She can do that?" asked Nash.

"Apparently, she has learned temporal manipulation. It doesn't mean she has mastered it, which is good. I still have my head."

"What happens when she masters it?" asked Ray. "Can she go back in time and like kill Hitler?"

"In a word: yes. But it also means she can go back and do anything she wants. She has all the power of the bloodstream at her disposal."

"And that's a lot of power," added Cleo. "What's your plan?"

"First, we have to get Oni protected."

"I can't tattoo dragon skin," said Nash."

"It's not really dragon skin," Oni floated over to Nash and brushed his face with his tail. "See? It's like a very soft satiny fabric. Silky. Sensual, some would say."

"I can't tattoo silk either."

"Yes, but you can draw it on a piece of fabric and we can sew it to Oni's tail," proposed Fletcher. "That would work, right?"

"I don't see why not," thought Nash. "I need to draw it with the enchanted ink I use for protection runes. We need to do it quick. The Wire will pick up on his appearance if they are in the area. And we pretty much know they are here looking for us."

"The assassination attempts on PJ and Kendall would be evidence," said Fletcher facetiously.

Nash went over to his tattoo station and looked through some drawers. They were all filled with various supplies like disposable needles and ink. Another drawer revealed plastic ink cup liners while another held latex safety gloves. He poured a small amount of enchanted ink into a cup.

Cleo had left and returned with a few scraps of cloth. "How about these?" She handed him a swatch that had a faded Hello Kitty on it. "I was going to try a new hobby. I was going to start quilting, but I did like two squares and gave up."

"You were making a Hello Kitty blanket?" asked Nash.

"Just shut up and take it." Cleo pushed it into Nash's hands. "I will sew it on his tail."

"I have to improvise. I don't have quill or old school ink pen." Nash grabbed a Sharpie from his stuff and dipped it in the inkwell. "This sharpie is totally dead and dried out. I should have thrown it away a long time ago, but I didn't."

She looked around the place, "I will help you declutter this if we live."

"Deal," Nash smoothed the swatch on his side workspace. "Now let's hope this works." He made the first line and was pleased. "That's good. Just the right amount of ink." He finished the last few strokes and began to blow on it to help it dry.

"How long will it be until it's dry?" Cleo readied a needle and thread. "We have to get this on Oni, ASAP. Or we will all be discovered."

"It's fine. Once the lines of the patterns set—it is active. You can sew it on now."

Cleo took the swatch, her needle, and scissors to the couch and sat. "Oni, come here."

Oni zipped over to her and dangled his tail in her lap. "Here it is. Will it hurt?"

"You won't feel a thing." Cleo began to stitch. "See?"

EPISODE SEVEN

The New Kids in Town

Compeer White Eyes stirred extra cream and sugar in his coffee as he and his two compatriots sat in a diner in Philadelphia. White Eyes was never sent into the field anymore, but he was this time. Wire associates called each other "Compeer" as a formal moniker instead of the historical "mister" since many Wire agents were not male nor quite human. His compeers Benedicta and Franz sat across from each other in the booth. Compeer White Eyes sat on the end in a stainless-steel chair with mid-century red vinyl and shiny upholstery tacks.

"You know that much sugar will end up killing you," commented Compeer Benedicta, a middle-aged European woman with thin black hair that grew thinner by the day.

"Yeah, how can you even see how much you put in there?" asked Compeer Franz—a white-blonde, older Nordic looking man.

White Eyes looked at them, not really, he just aimed his white cataract eyes in their direction. "I can smell how much sugar is on the spoon. I know how much it weighs. I know by the sound of the cream blooping into my coffee exactly how much I put in. It is a specific tone that only lasts 2 seconds." He stirred the cup, "When you have no sight your other senses get better."

"Pity you gave your sight to find *newbornes*," said Benedicta. "I wouldn't have done that."

"You are not committed to the cause?" He sipped his coffee.

"I am, but I like to go to the movies, and look at boys," she replied.

"Compeer Franz, do you think it unfortunate that I gave my sight up for the power to detect *newbornes*?"

"No, but I'm with Compeer Benedicta. I like the movies. And cute boys."

"While you two grin stupidly at each other," White Eyes sighed, "...yes you are that predictable, we have to pick up the trail again. I could see thin streams of the bloodstream, but I am afraid it has gone cold again."

"I bet they cloaked whomever so we couldn't find them and snuff them out," said Franz, fiddling with the lethal wire coiled within his watch.

"That would be standard operating procedure," said White Eyes. The waitress came back and put his omelet down in front of him. "Thank you, dear. It sure smells good." She put the other plates in front of the other two and left without saying anything. "Eat up, we have a busy day."

"Without a lead, we are just wasting our time here," Franz shoveled hash browns in his mouth like a heathen.

"Honestly," said Benedicta, "were you raised in a barn? Can you eat like someone with manners?"

"I'm hungry," he said while chewing. "We have been on useless stakeouts all over this city. Meanwhile more of our compeers in Detroit have died. Two were killed in a parking garage."

White Eyes toyed with his food, "Only one was killed by a

person. The other was ripped in half." He pointed at the TV screen. The volume was so low to the others, but he heard it. "That's who killed our compeer. The Hammer of the Universe."

Benedicta laughed, "Bullshit. That is just a legend."

"Like gods?" mused White Eyes who took a bite of his eggs. "Those are real."

"Point taken," she said. "So, what's the plan?"

"I think we should retrace the lingering bloodstream traces. I picked them up not too far from here."

"That godforsaken drag bar? We checked that out thoroughly," said Compeer Franz.

"There was a *newborne* there, I would stake my reputation on it," said White Eyes. "Have I ever been wrong before? Why do you think this is the first time in ten years I have been dispatched to the field? And that I was paired with two of the best assassins in the service."

"Thank you for that," blushed Benedicta. "I try."

"I wasn't complimenting you. I don't play with silly politics like that. Stating fact."

Franz drank some more coffee. "It sounds as good as any plan, I figure. It is so odd that a strong lead would just fizzle out."

"Agreed, something else is involved. I don't know what it is, but I will figure it out." White Eyes took a bite, "I always figure it out."

"We're not going in first, are we?" asked Franz.

White Eyes laughed, "Of course not, we send in pawns for that. We will gage the enemy's 'worth' by their performance."

"What if they kill the unknown god?" asked Benedicta. "I kind of enjoy that part."

"I doubt this one is a child or teenager," reminded White Eyes. "If they get a kill it will go on their record, and perhaps they will be promoted. Until then, no sense in taking a chance until we see what we're up against."

"Good thinking," complimented Franz.

"Do I ever do anything but?" White Eyes finished his coffee and turned his attention to his breakfast. "I am hungry now."

Pascal waited for darkness to fall before he left the safety of the grotto. He checked through his backpack full of odd equipment. There were still gaps in the story. He wanted to find out for Sarah so she had all the information she could have about her family.

"It looks like you're going somewhere," asked Sarah from behind. "Are you leaving?"

He glanced up at her from his task, "I have some more work to do."

"What kind of work?" she asked. "You don't have to. It's over. We are leaving after Truly's show. Don't you want to go with us?"

He paused, sighed, and turned. "I am not satisfied with what I know. I know what the other Sarahs told me, but can I really trust them? They are all 3D prints."

"So am I and you trust me."

"I'm sorry, I didn't mean that. I know you. You are the most human person I've ever met." He touched her face tenderly, "I think of you as my own kid, you know?"

Blushing, she averted her eyes. "I know. You're better than my dad that's for sure. Like a cool older brother." She watched him continuing to confirm all his belongings, "Pascal, what will my father do about me? About you?"

He paused and considered pretending not to hear the question. "I don't know."

"What are they like?" asked Sarah. "The other…me's."

"They look, talk, and act just like you. All of them are older than you. You are the last of them. I guess he felt he got it right."

"It doesn't feel right. It feels like a science fiction movie or something on Netflix."

He laughed, "I suppose you're right about that."

"You never said really what you're going to do. I mean, I get that you're going to look for more answers, but don't we know enough? What else could there be?" Sarah grabbed his hand and his attention, "Just come with us to Detroit. Forget all this."

"I wish I could, and I promise I will not be far behind. I know where you will be. I know Phineas Fletcher and his assistant Jesse Nash. They are good guys and you will be safe until I can get there. I won't let you down."

"You never have before," said Sarah.

"You go with the witch and Kendall. Allison has been cloaked and you won't be detected by the Wire. No doubt they are here in Philadelphia. And that Truly…she's a force. I think you will be safe on the trip."

"Promise me that you won't be long," urged Sarah. "I need to know that you're safe, too. I don't know what I would do without you."

"You're stronger than you know," he said. "I think you are destined to do great things, sweetheart. With or without me there, you will be an amazing woman."

"You should go then." She gave him a kiss on the cheek. "See you in Detroit?"

"Of course," he replied. "When are you guys leaving?"

"Truly wants to give a final performance at the drag bar she used to work at," said Sarah. "I really don't get it."

"You've had a sheltered life," said Pascal. "There are so many millions of different kinds of people out there. You will love it. Promise you will call me…" then he thought again. "Maybe not from the road or Detroit. My phone or yours may be compromised. Just find a way to call me."

"I promise," she said. "I gotta go, she wants to leave so she can prepare for what she called the 'fiercest farewell and birth all at the same time.' Don't ask me what that means."

"Yeah, that's a little weird," he agreed. "Go now, I have a few things to do then I am out of here. I am going to try and get into your dad's office at the hospital and find out more about this test people are taking."

"I think I failed the test," confessed Sarah. "They gave it to me the last time I went to get a check-up. And then the last time you took me for a check-up it was at a different place. I think they were trying to get me."

"Yes, I think that's what happened. That's why I want to find out more. It sounds cruel and unethical—to lock people up because they 'might' do something in the future? That is fucked up. Now go!" He waved her away.

Sarah walked off through the grotto that swallowed her up and closed behind her. Pascal watch her disappear, followed by the sound of many voices. There were laughs; Pascal picked out one of them fondly, passionately. Janelle had an unmistakable, rich laugh that was not ashamed to be heard. Lips that demanded to be kissed. Pascal followed the sound for they would be heading for the door, but not too closely. He wanted them to leave.

He walked through the grotto, admiring the flowers and butterflies. There was an unusual abundance of bumblebees, but he gave it no other thought. Indeed, it was a magical place. Same temperature year-round, snow if you wanted it, plenty of food, and water. Pascal wanted to taste the water for himself, just once. He knew Janelle and her sisters were Pierian maidens. Therefore, the mysterious Pierian Spring had to be close.

Pascal wondered around and lost track of time. Had it been 10 minutes or 10 hours? He sat on some nearby stones to rest. He wondered if he was just walking in big circles and that there really was no fountain. But what about Janelle? Why would she be here of all places if it weren't for the spring? The spring had to be close.

He focused, pushing out invasive thoughts that were sabotaging his efforts. Calling back to his Teutonic training, Pascal targeted his goal: find the fountain. He sucked in a deep breath and counted calmly letting it out. Pascal repeated the exercise over and over again. Slowly, his heart rate diminished, and his blood pressure subsided.

Then, Pascal heard the soft sound of water. It was close.

Nothing crazy, no waves, no agitation. The sound was subtle, and only suggested that there was a possibility of water being near. He feared perhaps he was hallucinating. The spring had ways of protecting itself on top of the Pierian maidens. Fear squeezed his eyes shut. What if it weren't there and it was only a cruel trick?

Pascal opened his eyes. In front of him appeared the stone well that held the spring's waters, which was calm and smelled of seaweed and salt. Above him, birds of every feather circled. For the first time in years, Pascal was frightened. He extended his arm and held out a begging palm. One step, two steps, ten steps until he touched the stones with his feet and stopped. Pascal looked down into the placid pool. His own handsome reflection returned a smile and a wink.

"What do I get if I touch you?" he asked aloud. There was no answer from anyone. "And cup my hands and bring your water to my lips?"

The reflection remained. Pascal studied his own face. Long eyelashes and thick brows complemented deep brown eyes. Flawless light brown skin and the shadow of stubble. A strong jawline. Black hair.

"I don't know who you are," Pascal said to the reflection. "You look like I used to be, but I don't think I am you anymore." He hesitated to touch the fountain, "I know the legends of the spring. If I drink from you I will receive clarity and truth, but in whatever form the universe desires."

Suddenly, the reflection broke from the confines of its owner. "Go ahead and do it."

"Did you just talk?" he asked. "It must be a trick, some protection magic."

"Nonsense and you know it," said the reflection. "I am the Pierian Spring, and this is what you wanted: truth and clarity. We have always known that. We have never strayed from our commitment and loyalty. We are protectors, through and through. Now, we must protect the Spring."

There was loud banging on the door, followed by the sound of drilling and more pounding.

"They are almost through the steel door," said the reflection. "They are not normal humans. They are bad, bad people."

"Recall the maidens, they will take care of them."

"There is no time," said the reflection and he glanced up at the whirring gyre of birds. "We must relocate to a safe place now. We must guard the Spring."

"I have to watch over Sarah," said Pascal. "I am the only one who has her best interests at heart. I know there is so much more to discover that she will need to know."

"Why does she need to know anything more than she does now? It won't change what she is, or who she thinks she is."

"What about the other Sarahs?"

"What about them?" retorted the reflection. "They've secured their father's entire empire and are secretly in control of it. They are allies and will make their presence known in time."

"No, I don't believe you. This is a trick."

"I am you. I am not saying anything you don't already know. I speak the truth because that is what you desire. You know we are protectors, and right now the spring needs us. It cannot relocate without someone to guard against undesirables who wish to use us."

"Those people trying to get in?" Pascal gestured to the growing din of drilling.

"They're trying to bust down the door, of course they're bad." The reflection raised his cupped hand and water leaked out of his tightened fingers.

Pascal's own hand mirrored the reflection and raised to his lips. He did not hesitate and sipped up the magic water. Then, he dug down deep and got a heartier drink. Above him, the cacophony of birds schooling like fish was deafening. The ground rumbled and broke along fault lines. Trees trembled and shed their leaves in torrents. Instinctively, Pascal climbed upon the stones and got into the water. Moments later, the whole of it all was swallowed by the earth.

The drills and hammers broke through the steel security door. Into the space walked Compeer White Eyes, Benedicta, and Franz. They scanned the darkened space warily. The harsh sodium streetlights poured through broken windows.

"It's empty," observed Benedicta who turned on a powerful flashlight. "There is nothing here. No gods, nothing."

"I guess you're losing your touch," grinned Franz.

White Eyes scanned the place crammed with old boxes and rusted, dilapidated car wash parts. "A god was here, and the trail is unmistakable. But there was something else here." He knelt and picked up a handful of dead leaves. "I don't know what, but something powerful was here."

"What about the god?" asked Benedicta. "He? She? They?"

"Hard to tell," he replied. "But not far from here. Phone the field agents and give them the vicinity and directions of this area. Tell them to be ready to move in when we find them. Keep them on the phone."

"On it," Benedicta was already dialing.

"Let's go," said White Eyes.

Truly stood at the DJ booth in a small room with a window that overlooked the stage at Mama Cane's. She had expected some nerves, but she was unusually calm. A performance usually caused anxiety just before the show, but once she was onstage it all melted away. The audience already loved her as Truly Scrumptious the drag queen, but now she had done more than transition: she was a goddess.

"Listen carefully, Adam," she was addressing the DJ. She handed him a flash drive, "Do not deviate at all on my next number. Turn on the auto strobes and pump out that fog. I don't care what you do with the lasers, but the strobes can't stop."

"Okay, that sounds weird. What if the audience starts having epileptic seizures?"

Truly glared at him through heavy, dramatic make-up and false eyelashes at least 2 inches long. "They aren't going to have seizures." She sighed, "I tell you what, do what I ask and you can have all the tips."

"All the tips?" he smiled. "You sure? You rake it in."

"I won't be needing it where I am going," she said. "Now here is a card. I wrote my introduction. Read it verbatim before you start the music."

"What's verbatim mean? Is that sexual?"

"No, Adam. It means read it word-for-word like I wrote it. Do not deviate. Do not make anything up like you sometimes do. Got it?"

He looked at it, reading the brief few sentences. "Your final performance?"

"Yes."

"And you have other performers that will be joining you for a very special, unforgettable story." He paused. "I don't think we have a budget to pay them, Truly."

"They're volunteering," she said. "Now do it. I'm going backstage." She walked a few steps down the staircase that led to the DJ booth, but paused. "Adam, please, it's my last show."

"I got you," he smiled. "Go. You've got five minutes."

Truly smiled and hurried down the stairs. She snaked backstage and found her mark just behind the part in the main curtain. Then she heard the music die and Adam began to speak.

"Ladies and gentlemen, thank you for coming to Mama Cane's, the best drag bar on the east coast!" There was a roar of applause, whistles, and cheers. "Make sure you get your tips and a drink ready because you are gonna love this next number. It is none other than our own Truly Scrumptious!" Then he read the prepared card: "Tonight is Truly's last performance here at Mama Cane's" There was audible disappointments. "Please get ready for one hell of a show you will never forget. Truly has worked very hard on this final number and will be joined on stage with some very special guests. So enjoy the choreography, the music, and the whole experience: *Heaven Must Have Sent You,* baby! THAT IS TRULY SCRUMPTIOUS!"

The automated strobes throbbed in perfect time with the military snare drum slamming on every sixteenth note. The kick drum and bass line followed as the melody of the deep church bells hit on every quarter note. Stepping out, Truly Scrumptious commanded the stage. Her thigh-high white stiletto boots slammed in time on the stage as she stalked like a super model down the catwalk in Paris. She interpreted every lyric, every sigh, every syllable without hesitation. Truly oozed confidence like the dense fog from the machines on the side of the stage. Her white catsuit hid nothing from the audience.

I've cried through many endless nights
A faux eye rub while vamping in time.
Just holding my pillow tight
Arms crossed one at a time over her chest. Fluttering those long false eye lashes.

Then you came into my lonely days
Pausing to hip sway, following the shape of her breasts with her manicured hands.

With your tender and your sweet ways
The staccato snare bled into a hard disco crush. The infection of Truly's energy spread through the clapping audience. Swirling lasers flashed from the supports above the stage. Everyone was on their feet. She strutted in time, pausing to whip her hair over her shoulder before raising her arms high to lip synch the lyrics. As she did, she spotted them in the audience. Out-of-place suits. The men who desperately wanted to join her on stage. With no cloaking rune, she had drawn them out just as planned. Time to meet Truly.

Now I don't know where you come from, baby
She pointed directly at two of them and invited them forth with seductive finger rolls.

Don't know where you've been, my baby
They obliged and approached the stage as she vamped backwards, leading them onto the catwalk.

Heaven must have sent you into my arms
One man stepped upon stage left while the other came up stage right. Truly smiled, not missing a lyric, beat, or eyelash flutter. The fog filled the stage; strobes, like rapiers, sliced through it. The first man lunged for her, only to be shocked when she flickered and vanished. She appeared a split second later in front of him with a severe punch to the face.

Now in the mornin' when I awake
The audience roared with approval as he buckled to the stage ,and she kicked him off to the floor.

There's a smile upon my face
Indeed, there was as she turned her attention to the second man on her stage.

You've touched my heart with gladness
He pulled out the razor-sharp wire from the watch on his wrist and came for Truly.

Wiped away all my sadness
In the fog and lights, to the driving beat, Truly stalked towards him. She was unafraid.

So long I've needed love right near me, a soft voice to cheer me
He rushed Truly with the intent of slicing her slender throat,

but she predicted his move and reappeared to punch him in the face like the first one. The crowd went insane.

Heaven must have sent you, honey, into my life, ooh
The first guy recovered and was back up to help kill her. But Truly maneuvered, knocked him to the stage, and stabbed her stiletto through his eye socket. Never missing a beat. She paused and held up her arms victoriously. The crowd went berserk, thinking it was all theatrics, not understanding the events unfolding were all too real.

It's heaven in your arms, boy, it's the sweetness of your charms
Three others engaged and walked to the stage after watching their comrades so quickly dispatched. Truly smiled and enticed them. A thigh. A breast. Hair whip, and a purposeful stalk close to backstage. They formed a triangle around her; two drew knives and the third pulled out his wire.

Makes me love you more each day. In your arms I wanna stay
Truly didn't wait for them, she flashed forward, predicting where one of them with the knives would be. She kneed him hard in the nuts, bringing him to the floor wailing. The crowd whooped and clapped.

Wanna thank you for the joy you brought me
She took the knives and knelt. Underneath the fog and lights, the knives went in deep. A cloud of fresh fog obscured the view. Truly rose with them in her hands and struck a pose. The crowd went wild.

Thank you for the things you taught me
Across the club near the front door, she caught a glimpse of Janelle, Roxette, and Tiffany screaming and cheering. The next move was taught to her by Janelle in their brief training sessions—a deadly spot-on double knife throw that knocked

the poor guy who tried to slice her throat with a wire off the stage.

Thank you for holding me close, when I needed you the most
Predicting the actions of the two remaining attackers, Truly went down on one knee. Slashing left, slicing right, she severed one Achille's tendon in each. The crowd came to the stage and showered it with tips. Many finger-snapped their riotous approval. Hoots and howls nearly drowned out the music.

Now I don't know much about you, baby
Truly was vamping in time with the music once again. Hips rocking and swaying. Boots cracking through to the center of the planet. In her mind she tallied her victories: two were probably dead; two couldn't walk; and she couldn't quite remember what she did to the first guy. Her senses were crazy. Truly's instincts were screaming, there was another man still in the audience. One left. Come on. Let me see you.

But I know I can't live without you
He had a gun, though. He aimed and fired. Truly already knew where that bullet was going and flashed out of the way safely. The crowd howled with approval as Truly seemed to flicker in one spot and magically reappear six feet away. She must be an illusionist and a drag queen. Truly laughed to herself. The gunman was still out there and he could hurt someone innocent. Focus.

Heaven must have sent you. To love only me, ooh
Improvising, Truly did hip thrusts with forward steps and windmill arms towards the stage edge. She tracked the audience for him. He would reveal himself. He wouldn't be jumping and dancing, so she locked on to a solitary man taking aim with a gun. She predicted that.

It's heaven in your arms

Dazzling everyone with her 'trick' Truly flashed forward just as the trigger was going to be pulled. She intercepted his arm, brought it down hard on the bar. Truly wasn't sure if it was his bones or the bar that made the cracking sound. The crowd went wild, showering Truly with tips. She took the gun and danced triumphantly to the stage.

Boy, it's the sweetness of your charms

She turned to see him holding his arm and zombie-walking behind her to the stage. Her first encounter with the Wire. Six up. Six down. No innocent bystanders, just cheering crowds. Maybe she should have tried this kind of show earlier, she laughed out loud.

Makes me love you more each day

In her mind, Truly flashed ahead in prediction. He could still use his good arm to pull out his wire. As he made it up the stairs behind her, Truly decided she didn't need to move using her ability when she could take him on her own. The strobes flashed with the beat. Fog rolled along the floor. The crowd was pumping and raining dollars down on the stage. Truly Scrumptious jammed her heel down hard on his foot, then she ducked and whirled until she was behind him instead. She reached high and took his weakened arms in her hands. With her newfound abilities was newfound strength, and Truly wrapped the wire around his own neck. Then, Truly Scrumptious ended her final number with a deathdrop that severed the head of the Wire agent. The crowd lost its mind. The show went on.

In your arms I wanna stay

Today was the day that Truly Scrumptious came to slay.

EPISODE EIGHT

Misfit Toys

PJ already forgot what time was. She looked down in the basket at the strange swatches with moving pictures on them and took one out. Her blanket was growing as was the task given to her by Pluto, God of the Underworld. There weren't many left to be added.

The one in her hand was interesting. It was of a castle that looked like a dragon stretching its neck to the sky. The spines and scales formed a high wall of red bricks that spiraled outward through a village offering protection to the inhabitants. Flags along the wall blew in the breeze. She held it close and sniffed it, lilacs.

Just as she was about to begin stitching it onto her blanket with the magic thread of the Fates, she heard soft footsteps coming toward her. PJ paused and looked up to see a stooped elderly woman making her way from somewhere deep inside the labyrinth. When she arrived, she simply stood and looked PJ up and down with unabashed judgment.

She smacked her gums, "Are you enjoying your task?"

"What's to enjoy, it's sewing," said PJ.

The old woman cackled. "This is going to be a long eternity for you. And probably me."

"Why you?"

Instead of answering, the old woman snatched the blanket from PJ with surprising nimbleness. She held it close to her eyes, inspecting it. PJ observed, not really knowing what to think or how to react. Who was this old crone? She hadn't seen any other people in the Underworld since she had arrived except Phineas Fletcher. She searched her own memory to make sure she wasn't fooling herself. No, PJ couldn't remember any other people.

"Excuse me," PJ said. "Who are you?"

The old woman tossed the blanket back at PJ, "Good needlework. Pluto was right that you would do well at Shadow Work."

"What is that?"

"Shadow Work?" She cackled again. "It's what we all do down here. Do you think we are here for our health? This is where fate is crafted. Where did you think it happened? Heaven?"

"I've never thought about it at all," said PJ.

"That's obvious."

"There is no need to be rude," said PJ. "It's not even fair that I am here. I am a victim."

"You enjoy that delicious slice of delusion, dear. I will come back later and check on you."

"No, wait, what does that even mean?"

The old woman paused and sighed. "This is it. This is where you are. You can moan and have all the self-pity you want. Those things don't fly down here. Maybe your mother would give you a nice pat and an 'Oh, there there' but that's not here."

PJ shoved her blanket in the basket. "Fine. I'm done with this. I refuse to finish. I don't care who says I have to. I will find a way out. I don't deserve being here anyway. I was attacked by some monster."

"And saved by Pluto," the old woman reminded her. "You are in debt to him."

"Then I will find a way to pay him off," she said defiantly.

Again, the old woman laughed. "Maybe you're just too stupid to realize he may have already given you that." She looked down at the blanket shoved in the basket.

"The blanket?" PJ fished it out, "If I finish this he will let me leave?"

"I never said that," she smiled, five teeth remained. "That's your delusion speaking again."

"Who are you? Why are you torturing me?"

"I came to inspect your stitches. They are careful and perfectly spaced. Why don't you finish this by the time I return to get you."

"Get me?"

"Do you think this is where the beloved favorite of the Prince of Shadows would end up?"

"The Prince of Shadows? Professor Fletcher?"

"The one who walks above and below, yes that one." She started to walk away again, "Finish and we will talk about your future."

"There's such a thing as a future down here?"

"If you want one."

It was the last thing the old woman said before she hobbled off into the labyrinth of the Underworld.

Janelle and her sisters safely evacuated Truly and the others out the back door of the strip club. It was chaos inside. Only now were the patrons and staff figuring out that there were dead men, and Truly murdered them all in the span of three minutes and twenty-two seconds—including the fade out.

Truly ruminated on the events that just occurred. There was

a gnawing in her heart. She was a murderer now for sure. Only days ago, that fact bothered her immensely. Truly analyzed her feelings about killing the doctor with the plastic gun. He deserved it. He was dangerous and predatory. Weren't the Wire agents the same? Their goal was to kill new gods, and sow animosity with false religion among humans. Was she any different than them? They murdered. She murdered.

"Hurry," said Janelle. "We have to get out of here quickly. The cops won't be far behind." She snapped her fingers at Truly who seemed to be in a trance. "Earth to Truly."

"Worse, the Wire is already here," added Tiffany.

"Didn't I kill them all?" asked Truly, coming back to the present.

Roxette sighed, "You never can kill them all, unfortunately."

"I am having conflicting feelings about killing them, to be honest," said Truly.

"Don't," replied Janelle. "They would not afford you the same sympathy. Remember, they gave up their humanity a long time ago. Some of them aren't even human."

"I understand that, but does killing them make me any better than them?"

"I said you can't afford to think like that," said Janelle. "That is how doubt gets into your mind. It will make you hesitate and that is when you are vulnerable. Push all of that out of your mind right now."

"What's the plan?" interrupted Kendall and changing the subject. "Our SUV is here but I don't think I can fit everyone in it."

"We are not going," said Janelle. "We must stay and protect the Pierian Spring."

"We need you with us," said Sarah. "Pascal will be coming, I'm sure of it. You should come, too."

"No, we must get back. We will equip Pascal with food and supplies before he leaves to join you."

"What was so important that he had miss the show?" asked

Truly. "I totally killed it in there." Kendall smiled and they high-fived. "You know it, gurl."

"All that is going to do is piss them off," said Poppy.

"The world needed to know I was here," said Truly. "They should think twice about trying anything again."

"They don't reason like that," the witch explained. "They have one goal: kill gods so they can stay in charge with their lies. They've done it for thousands of years. Do you think a killer drag queen who takes out a few of them will deter them? You have your wig glued on too tight."

"It's not a wig."

Poppy sighed, "Whatever."

"Enough talking, let's move." Janelle walked over to the SUV, "This one is yours?" The kids nodded. "Poppy, can you check it for curses and bombs?"

"I already did," she said. "I put a few enchantments on it, too. We will be hard to track. Truly, sure you don't want some kind of cloaking rune or spell?"

"No, I won't hide anymore," she said. "I'm done with that."

"Even if it means the rest of us won't die?" asked Kendall.

"The whole vehicle is cloaked," Poppy said. "When we get in, we'll be invisible to whatever they use to find us."

"How do they do it, do you think?" asked Allison.

"That is a mystery," Janelle looked back at the open back door to the club. It was chaos, "Go, now."

Kendall drove with Truly in the passenger seat. Poppy, Allison, and Sarah piled in the back seat, and all looked back as the Rogue pulled away. Janelle sighed. The taillights shrank in the distance and made a left turn that led to the highway. They were on their way.

"We must get back to the Spring," she said. "It makes me nervous that the Wire is so close."

"We have to get back for our own protection. No doubt there are more Wire agents in the city. Now that Truly has killed some of them, she will be a top target," commented Roxette as they walked the side streets to the garage only a few blocks away.

"Are we safe?" asked Tiffany.

"Once we get inside they won't be able to find us," Janelle said.

"Good, I do not wish to lose any more sisters," said Roxette. "May I suggest we not walk? It will take too much time and I feel exposed."

Janelle nodded and stopped in a darkened area between two old buildings. There, the sisters transformed into elegant white birds and took to the sky. In a matter of minutes, they flew to the car wash and returned to their naked human forms. However, something was not right. The metal gate over the entrance was up.

"Stop," ordered Janelle. The others noticed the door, too. She looked around and found a hunk of pipe. "Stay close."

"Look," pointed Tiffany, "Pascal's car is still here."

"Never mind that now," said Janelle, her senses sharp.

In a protective triad formation, the sisters crept into the maw of the old car wash. What had been familiar and safe before, was now a terrifying tunnel. The brushes loomed like giant silhouettes. Wire agents could be behind any of them waiting for the right moment to strike. Deeper inside they went. Water dripped, critters rustled, the raw streetlights invaded the space through broken windows. They arrived at the steel security door—the only barrier between the Pierian Spring and the mortal world. It stood open, twisted and gouged. The spring was gone.

"NO!" yelled Janelle.

"It's gone!" screamed Roxette.

"What do we do?" asked a panicked Tiffany.

Janelle calmed herself and looked around the place. "It's true. The Pierian Spring left us behind. We were the guardians."

"Do you think the Wire breached the door?" asked Tiffany.

"That could only happen if the magic left and it was returned to an ordinary door," she replied. "It must have sensed imminent danger, sisters."

"And Pascal, do you think he was in here when it happened?" asked Tiffany.

"I would bet on it," answered Roxette. "His car is outside. He never leaves that car anywhere."

Janelle stood tall. "We will find the Spring again. We will never give up. But now, we must join Truly and protect them on their way to Detroit. Perhaps, this is a new chapter for us."

"But how?"

"It's too far to fly, and I am no Canada Goose."

"Let's go in and get some clothes, that is the first order," said Janelle.

The sisters entered the dilapidated office and storage area of the car wash. They located some suitcases they kept old clothes in for an emergency, and this was an emergency. Then, they went back outside.

"Follow me," Janelle said to them.

Janelle saw the beautiful sports car beneath the streetlights and walked over to it. She studied it carefully, looking for a way to get inside. Janelle got down on her back and slid slightly beneath the driver's side door. With her hand she felt around as if she expected something hidden. Then her hand gripped around a magnetic, metallic key holder. It was very difficult to remove.

"He would never leave without his precious car," said Tiffany.

"I agree," said Janelle, pulling herself out and stood. "He was paranoid about locking himself out and hid an extra key. I only know about it because he did just that when he took me on a picnic."

"When did you go on a picnic with him?" Roxette asked. "Sister has secrets."

"It wasn't a secret," she unlocked the driver's side door, "we just didn't feel the need to tell anyone. Now get in. We are going to follow them and make sure they get to Detroit. Then we will find the Pierian Spring wherever it has manifested and return to our roles as guardians."

The three of them got in the Maserati Levante. Janelle started it up and grinned as the engine purred like a tiger ready to pounce. She revved it a few times, slammed it into gear, and sprayed the street with gravel.

The contrast in the weather surprised Calliope as the bitter wind coming off the straights of the northern Scottish coast stung any exposed flesh. She started the journey back to civilization more than a day ago, stopping at small villages friendly to the new goddess. Word travelled fast amongst the followers after the massacre. Did she really kill the Ancient One? Calliope wasn't sure if the creature was killed, but the wedding was cancelled along with the lives of most of the collected followers. Those that survived, and Lady Dolce, made sure word travelled ahead of Calliope. Safe passage was assured as any new disciples painted a yellow star on their doors. Calliope liked the star and thought it made a perfect symbol for herself.

The hidden island was so much warmer and agreeable than the bitterness of the northern Scottish coast. She wondered how ancient people lived and could tolerate such uncomfortableness. Calliope hated to be uncomfortable, and her new followers equipped her with handmade wool sweaters and scarves to keep her warm.

As she looked out over the water and the growing coastline, three familiar large black birds settled on the ferry's deck. The few people that were on it marveled at them and their apparent lack of fear of human beings. The three hopped closer and closer to Calliope, but stopped just short of being under foot.

"Hi," she looked down at them, their black eyes flickered instead of blinked. "I was wondering where you three were." One cawed loudly, startling her. "Please, no divinations here. I don't think I could explain it."

Instead, her oracles waited silently on the deck next to her. Their bodies seemed to float while their legs went up and down with the motion of the rocky waves. Calliope wondered what was in store for her now that she chosen to return to the world. Lady Dolce would not join her no matter how Calliope begged her. She hated modern human civilization, but did like the term 'Shade.' Calliope grew fond of Lady Dolce and trusted her. It was the first time in a long time that Calliope felt that an adult actually cared about her. Lady Dolce thought she could be something great.

"She thinks I am a star," laughed Calliope to her birds. "I wish I could see me the way she does." She sighed. "We'll know soon enough. I wonder if anyone has been looking for me." Calliope looked down at them, really her only loyal companions. "I seem to fuck things up, don't I?" They just looked at her and blinked their eyes.

The Scottish mainland was closing in. There were few fellow passengers on the ferry from the remote islands. She wondered how many people actually knew about the Ancient One and the story of the girl who exploded like the sun. How far had the rumors travelled? Calliope didn't recall seeing anyone with phones to video the event. She would soon find out, though. All she had to do was look for the yellow star to find the folks who believed in her instead of the cephalopod god.

EPISODE NINE

There Once Was a Girl Who Had Enough

Standing 500 feet from the riverbank brought back so many memories for Carmen. All of them were bitter, terrifying, the seed of her revenge. *Rio Bravo del Norte*, the Rio Grande River as colonizers called it. Carmen was not alone as she contemplated her next move. La Llorona stood by her, face exposed and decorated like a traditional Day of the Dead sugar skull.

"This is where the nightmare began," said La Llorona, the warm desert wind lifting her lacey shawl that covered a black taffeta dress.

"No, you're wrong," said Carmen and she looked over at her spectral companion, hood pulled over and covering most of her face. Was the entity really next to her? She was like a ghost that had not fully manifested. "Why are you here with me?"

"I have been with you since the beginning," she replied. "I answered your pleas that day your family was slaughtered."

"Why did you even come? I am sure there are many children calling out for relief from abuse."

"You are special," she replied. "You are the Hammer of the Universe. I felt it but was not sure. You needed my guidance."

"The Hammer," she scoffed. "I have the ability now to get my revenge, and so much more. But how right is that? Part of me questions the decisions I have made and the future I have planned for myself."

"Listen to yourself," argued La Llorona. "The voice questioning your ethics is not yours. It is the remnants of Nemesis. And all the Hammers before you. Remember, all those that have hosted the Hammer's power have died."

"Nemesis isn't dead," countered Carmen, the hood hiding her eyes. "We have her in prison. I still don't know how that happened."

"You willed it," said her companion. "The universe manifests what you imagine. That is its power."

"Why didn't I kill her?"

"You cannot kill her. She is a persistent god. She is formidable. It would be hard to kill her, indeed."

"Is this power evil?" asked Carmen. "And why me?"

"It is not evil. It is nothing. It is what you, the Hammer, decide it will be."

"Then am I evil?"

"No, child. You are damaged. You have been wronged in the greatest of ways. Do you not remember standing on this riverbank when you were just a girl? Your family dead. Rotting in your village. An example to the community to not cross the drug lords."

"Then why haven't I focused my powers on finding and murdering them?"

"You will visit all of the ones who wronged you," stated La Llorona. "That is why I am with you, to offer you guidance."

Carmen laughed. "It's like I am a god like my friends, and you are my oracle."

"You don't need an oracle, and you are a god. The universe has given you unimaginable power to do what you wish. And you have chosen to cleanse evil—those that have wronged you. You were a victim over and over again. Those responsible will pay. But you may also help others that have gone through what you have and prevent the atrocities from happening again."

"Why should I listen to you? A ghost cursed to Hell for killing her own children in a jealous rage?"

"There is more to that story."

"Then, please enlighten me before I do this so I may understand the motivation."

"I was victimized, too." La Llorona stated. "The legends of my evil forget what drove me to my rage. I was provoked. My children were a product of rape. My husband forced himself on me with a fist and terror. Every time I looked at my children, I only saw his face. He loved them even though he still raped and beat me. Eventually, I was rendered barren from his beatings. I bled so bad I knew I could never have another child."

"I didn't know," said Carmen. "I'm sorry those things happened to you."

"I begged the devil for a just revenge. He put in my head the solution: I had to kill the faces that looked so much like my husband. I did not think about my own love for them, no matter how they were begotten. I wanted him to hurt. I wanted him to hurt forever."

"Killing him would do nothing to soothe your pain?"

La Llorona nodded. "I killed what he loved to cause him endless pain until he died. Unfortunately, in my rage I forgot my love for them, too. When the deed was done, after I had drowned them in this very river, I was damned. The universe cursed me with the thirst of motherhood, but also of revenge. I wanted the love of children, and my uncontrollable jealousy of any mother who still had their children, I answered the calls of any young child that called to me."

"You came to them, and then drowned them?"

"Yes, but they never could join me in the afterlife. I was childless no matter how many I took. That is part of my damnation. To be hungry and be able to eat but never satiated. I only succeeded in killing innocents, but I cannot stop because it was my penance for my deal I made on this riverbank that day."

"Until me?" asked Carmen. "Why didn't you just kill me as a child after what you saw what I was going through? I was nearly blind when the smugglers got me over the river. I was raped by them. All of them. I was too young to get pregnant. I just closed my eyes and I remember calling to you."

"I heard those calls, and I felt your destiny. I wanted to come to you, but it was not time. I had foreseen what you would bring to these men, all of them, for what they did to me. And you. All of us."

La Llorona turned to face Carmen. She turned Carmen towards her, and with slender white hands, pulled the hood off her face. Carmen's face was painted as La Llorona: white makeup with blackened eye sockets, illustrated teeth on her lips, and deep purple cavities contouring her cheekbones. Nothing needed to be said between them. La Llorona gave a slight, almost imperceptible nod. Carmen returned the affirmation, and then the specter turned to dust and blew away with the wind.

Carmen walked down to the river. In the foliage on the banks, there were a few desperate people hiding. She picked this crossing place on purpose: it was her crossing place. This is where she paid the price for the promise of freedom. Her mind forced all the memories to the front of her brain. She couldn't ignore them if she wanted to.

Just a few hundred feet separated Carmen from the riverbank. Across the river, she watched as three U.S. Border Patrol vehicles approached. They all stopped and got out. Carmen noticed razor wire coils along the ground and cameras on wooden poles lining the U.S. side of the Rio Grande. Several drones buzzed over the river and headed towards her.

"Don't be afraid," she said to the refugees hiding. "I will get you across."

They looked upon her with wonder and terror. They saw her makeup.

"La Llorona…" one of them whispered in Spanish.

"If that's who you see," she replied. "I will take you across."

"What price?"

She smiled, "No price at all. Helping right this wrong is payment enough."

Suddenly, a loud bullhorn with an English-speaking voice issued a warning. "This is United States property. Crossing this river is illegal. Do not attempt to cross the river. If you seek asylum go to the main crossing."

Carmen kept walking, ignoring their words. The warning came again. This time in Spanish. The border patrol agents lined up on the bank, rifles drawn, with military-trained dogs on leashes. She kept walking.

Carmen paused and looked behind her where she could see the refugees peering out from behind their hiding places at her. She held up her arm and motioned for them to join her. One by one they lined up behind the Hammer. She returned her attention to the riverbank.

The water was at her feet. She stood on a rocky outcropping with all the brush and trees trimmed away. This is where her smugglers raped her. This was where she paid to cross the river for a promise that never ripened.

The warnings continued. Carmen raised her hands and conjured the energy of the universe. Thick dark purple ribbons of energy rose, snaked across the river, then opened up revealing the bottom. The thick mud was the only barrier now between freedom and damnation.

"Go back!" shouted the bullhorn. "Discontinue using whatever weapon you have or we will be forced to open fire. This is your only warning!"

Carmen looked back behind and saw a row of at least fifty

people. Some were old, some were just children no older than when she tried to cross. The one difference was no smugglers or pirates were here to take advantage of them. And no one could save the border patrol agents from her crossing.

"Follow me," she said to them. "Do not be afraid. You will not sink in the mud. I will provide the path."

Carmen turned towards the river once more and resumed. As promised, the crack of rifles sent bullets whizzing across the river. The reaction was secondary, an impulse, something she was not even aware of. A curtain of the purple ribbon absorbed the bullets. The agents kept firing with no success. Carmen lifted her leg to take her first step across the exposed mud. As she put her foot down, instead of sinking in the muddy bottom, the purple energy radiated outward providing a solid surface. Every step and the surface remained behind her for the refugees to follow.

They made progress amid the shower of bullets. More agents pulled up, flanking to the left and right of the original group of border patrol agents. One fired past Carmen and the safety of the shield, striking one of the helpless immigrants. He fell dead as those around him screamed. The other new agents fired as well, hitting another refugee.

No, I will not be victimized ever again. We will not be victimized ever again.

Carmen's eyes washed with rage. From her body emanated a halo-shaped ribbon of the energy. Like a pebble dropping into a placid lake, the ripple carried through the air. It met no resistance, sharper than any razor, and sliced the agents in half at the chest. The tops of their vehicles were also decapitated. The dogs simply barked as the top half of their handlers plopped to the ground in front of them, still screaming because they hadn't yet bled out. That didn't take long, though.

The drones above whirred and circled, obviously taking video of the crossing. Carmen lifted a hand to destroy them, but she hesitated. No, let the world see this. Let them know what is coming. They will realize the Hammer has come to level them.

Kendall looked down at the gas gauge. They had been driving for a few hours without having to stop. He didn't want to stop either. He replayed the insane events of the last few months. It was all so absurd. Kendall glanced in the rearview mirror at the sleeping passengers in the back seat. It made him feel a little settled, he felt like he was finally doing something right.

Truly was the only other one awake. She was in the passenger seat and stared out into the night. Periodically, she offered to drive if he was too tired, but he said was okay. Driving made him feel like he was contributing to the group. They were all special.

"What are you thinking about?" Truly asked softly, not wanting to wake the others.

It surprised Kendall, "Uh, nothing really."

"I know when someone is preoccupied," she said. "I am the king of it…well the queen now."

"So true," they giggled together.

"So, you're the oracle to this guy named Ray?"

Kendall nodded and glanced at her before returning his attention to the dark road. "Yeah, it was poetic justice. He's the hottest guy in school, and really nice. A total boy scout. He didn't notice me at all until I had a fucking seizure as he walked by, and I had my first divination."

"That's embarrassing," commented Truly. "I can relate to wanting the guy you can't have."

"Yeah, it sucks. Ray has got to be the most genuine guy, though. Seriously, and Professor Fletcher is sure he is the rising king of the new gods about to take over the Earth."

"Take over the Earth?" Truly looked out the window as mile markers passed by. "How can they take over the Earth?"

"I don't mean take over," Kendall tried to clarify. "Do you

know the whole story of what's going on these days?"

"I've pieced most of it together from my time with the Pierians," she replied.

"Do you know about the old gods, too?"

"Old gods? Like Zeus and Thor?"

"Older than those. Apparently, gods come and go on Earth every once in a great while. Well, there are Ancient Ones, too. They want to be the only gods on Earth. You know, like HP Lovecraft and Cthulhu. Those Ancient Ones. We fought one."

"Really? That's real? I read a lot of Lovecraft when I was…a boy," said Truly. "What happened when you fought one?"

"It was so fucking intense," he said. "The monster couldn't beat Ray. Ray was just…*pow and zing*…with his power. He can make indestructible shields and make them into shapes. He is indestructible himself."

"Indestructible?" asked Truly. "That I'm not sure I believe. Everyone has a weakness."

"I don't know," continued Kendall. "Ray saved our asses until that thing started shrieking at this super high pitch. Everyone collapsed and it looked like we were done. My best friend PJ was killed."

"I'm sorry."

"It's okay, she isn't really totally dead. This is the part where it gets weird."

"It can't get much weirder than me drinking from a magic fountain and transitioning to my female persona."

"Really?" astonished Kendall. "That's fucking cool. Um, you wanted to transition, right?

"Yes, I knew one way or another that I was not in the correct body. It never felt like me. That's one of the reasons I invented Truly. I feel like me when I am Truly."

"And now you are truly—Truly." They laughed together. "And think of how much you saved in surgery."

"I hear that," smiled Truly. "It would have taken forever for me to save my tips. Then I shot that pervert psychiatrist in the head."

"Wow, really?"

"Yeah, he said I failed my test and I had to surrender myself to the authorities."

"I didn't fail my test," said Kendall. "Thank god."

"I had to escape and that's how I found the Pierians. And that's when I met Sarah and Allison. We got pretty close really quickly. I feel like I am supposed to protect them."

"Well, the way you dispatched those thugs back in the bar, that was awesome."

"Thanks, it went better than I planned honestly." Truly hesitated. "Can I tell you something and promise you won't judge?"

"I am a judgement-free zone," he grinned. "Go for it."

"I am having a lot of conflict after what I did at the show. Everyone thought it was staged, just part of the act, but I saw some of the faces in the crowd. A lot of them looked at me with…I don't know…"

"Fear? Disgust? Appalled?"

"Wow, those came to mind quickly."

"Sorry," Kendall focused on the road. "So, you don't know how you feel?"

"It isn't what I expected."

"Why?"

"It was so easy to do it—kill them. I kind of liked it, to be honest. I knew they were bad guys and all…" she took a deep breath, "…but they were babies once. A mom or a dad loved them. I mowed them down without a thought."

"That is rough," affirmed Kendall. "Sorry you are feeling like that. But from all I have seen and experienced, all the rules we followed as good human beings aren't really applicable anymore. I mean, you made it look like a dance. Or a movie fight scene."

"I could just see them in my mind and I went ahead of them a little in time, and caught them where they were going to be."

"I should forget trying to sneak up and surprise you?"

"Yeah, I don't think that would be a good idea."

Kendall pointed at a luminescent road sign signaling that gas and food was at the next exit. "I have to stop for gas. Hey," he addressed the girls in the back seat with a loud voice, "anyone have to pee? Or get a snack?"

Groggily, Sarah lifted her head. "I do."

Allison and Poppy also had to go.

"Okay, here are some ground rules," said Truly. "Don't get noticed. Don't make a scene. Just get in and out." Truly held out her hand to Kendall. "Give me some money and I will pay for the gas in cash. No credit card."

Kendall handed her a wad of cash, "Okay, I guess we can all go in. I will go pee first and you pay. Then I'll come out and pump while you guys do whatever."

They pulled off the exit and found the brightly-lit, 24-hour truck stop. Even though it was the dead of night, there were dozens of people fueling up. Kendall went to the men's room, while the others went for the women's room.

Truly went to the bullet-proof window separating the worker from the customers. "$50 on number 6."

The worker eyed Truly up and down, "Sure it will hold $50?"

"Yes, I am sure."

He took the money and punched in the amount and activated the pump, "There ya go little lady."

She wasn't really offended by the term the old man used for her. Truly walked towards the restroom just as Kendall was coming out. They high-fived and he went out to pump the gas. As she walked down the hall, she had the most imperceptible smile of victory on her lips. She pushed the women's bathroom door open and went in.

Outside, in the brilliant beams of the white LED lights, Kendall put the nozzle in the tank. His mind drifted. The dial on the pump rolled and ticked as gallon after gallon went in. The sloshing sound reminded him of flowing water. Then, he startled to awareness as a dark car pulled up to the gas station.

"Fuck," he whispered. "Please, just be normal people…please be normal people."

The dark sedan stopped opposite Kendall on the other side of the island. A man got out as well as an old woman wearing a *Live, Laugh, Love* sweatshirt. He sighed they were safe. No one could wear that and be an assassin.

"Nice night," she said walking by on her way to the gas station. "All these stars."

"Yes, it's really beautiful," replied Kendall.

The older man put in his credit card then pulled it out quickly. He paused as the pump activated. "Hey there, where you heading this late at night?"

"Oh, um, I'm driving to my dad's house."

"Where does he live?" the man asked.

Kendall got nervous and started making things up. "Um, he lives in Cleveland."

"You go to school here or something?"

Kendall nodded, "Yeah, I go to school here. Driving home 'cause he's kinda sick."

"Sorry to hear that, I hope he gets better soon."

They both got quiet. Kendall's pump rolled up and stopped at $49.55. He gave it a few extra squeezes until it stopped at 50.

"You shouldn't top it off like that," the man commented suddenly. "It could be a fire hazard."

"None spilled," said Kendall. "It's all good, thanks."

He got into the SUV and pulled it up into a parking spot to wait for the rest of them. One by one they came out. The only one left inside was Truly and the *Live, Laugh, Love* woman.

Then he saw Truly looking in a cooler for a drink. As she was making a selection, *Live, Laugh, Love* came out of the bathroom and instantly went to the cooler area. She had pulled a gun. A moment later, *Live, Laugh, Love* crashed through the window just as Truly flashed ahead a moment in time to intercept the attack.

"Oh my god!" shrieked Kendall. He tried to get out, but the

old man was out the driver's side window with a gun pointed at him through the glass.

He grinned to expose a mouthful of missing teeth, "No, no, no. There will be no running."

Truly leapt through the broken glass and snatched *Live, Laugh, Love* off the ground. She was dazed and bloody. The clerk was screaming. An alarm went off. No doubt the police were only minutes away.

"Here," said Truly, "you want her alive?"

"Not particularly," he said. "We just want you. Alive. Or dead. Preferably alive, but you are far too dangerous. You have gone viral with my colleagues. We are very intrigued by you. Go ahead and kill her if you want to. I will shoot him. You want him alive?"

Then around Truly's head, hovered Mico. They flirted and bounced, telling Truly something in her ear.

"What is that?" Asked the man as he lowered his gun. "A golden snitch?"

"Look carefully, I think you will figure it out—mister Wire guy," smiled Truly. "Mico, please take care of him."

There was a flash of metallic colors and a streak of rainbow light. It started from Truly's ear where Mico once was and passed through the old man's forehead. Mico was on the other side of his head, exiting from a hole in the back of his skull. The man was shocked, knowing what had happened but not quite believing it.

"Hummingbird assassin," smiled Truly. Then she threw *Live, Laugh, Love* onto the ground next to him. "She may be alive still, but you're not."

Truly got into the vehicle, "Let's get the fuck out of here now."

Kendall slammed it into reverse, then drive, and skidded out onto the dark highway towards Detroit.

Arranging transportation to the wrecked conclave of Old Livonia was much more of a challenge than Calliope thought.

At first, anyone she asked drew blank stares, even those who had gold stars on their property. It didn't help much that she was American. There was an instant suspicion of a lone girl traveling in Scotland. Calliope reminded herself that although she had been transformed by her experiences on the cult island, she still didn't have a proper passport. And no one would ever believe how she really came to be in Scotland.

Fewer and fewer gold stars were hanging on doors and in windows as she ventured further into civilization. Surely, there had to be someone who could help her. It was getting dark when she arrived in Aberdeen. Kind strangers who had gold stars helped her get that far. When she asked if they knew of any with gold stars in the large city, there was hesitation and ultimately, they said no. Calliope didn't believe them but thanked them anyway.

She decided to find a place to grab some food for it had been at least a dozen hours since she ate anything. None of the food was especially appealing. A gold star man and his wife dropped her off near the edge of the river Don. It was developed and there were a few nice bar/restaurants. Calliope liked the vibe and thought it needed another few years before it was really hopping. It was safe, though.

Her oracles had flown off on their own once they made it to the mainland. Rude, she thought, *my oracles were supposed to help me survive.* They just took to the sky and left her behind. They weren't much, but at least she didn't feel so alone when they were near. Then, they landed on a light pole over her head and gave their *ca-caw*.

"Did you hear me thinking about you? About time," she said. "Why don't you show me a way out of this town." They simply looked at her with their flash-blinking eyes and tilted heads. Then she noticed they were above the door of a small bar. "You guys are assholes," she said. The sign above the inconspicuous bar was The Gold Star.

Calliope opened the heavy, ancient wooden door. There

was no way to tell how old the establishment actually was, but Aberdeen was one of those queerly old European cities that had many secrets. Her entrance drew the eyes of the few patrons nursing their beers. The bartender looked up from his phone momentarily but seemed very uninterested in her appearance.

She went to the bar and sat on a rickety metal stool. "Hi," she said to the bartender. He didn't look up from his phone but returned the greeting. "Do you have food?" He didn't respond and she waited a second before saying it again. "Sir, do you serve food? I saw the gold star over the door."

Calliope got his attention with the mention of the star. "Yeah," he said with a brogue so thick it took a moment for her to understand the word. "We have bangers and mash, some blood sausage left."

She wrinkled her nose, "Anything more simple? Like fish and chips?"

He laughed, "Americans."

"What?" she smiled. "Yes, I am American. But don't hold that against me."

He put the phone down, smiled, and offered an extended hand. "Sorry, we don't get a lot of foreigners here at the Gold Star. I'm Bruce."

Calliope shook his hand and introduced herself. "So do you have something more…simple?"

"Yes, we have beef and ham sandwiches. Even we get tired of Scottish and British food."

"A ham sandwich sounds fantastic," she said.

"You want a beer to go with that?"

"A beer? I'm not 21."

Bruce laughed, "We really don't do that here. The drinking age thing. Do you want a beer? We have a nice house pale ale."

"I don't drink a lot," she said. "It won't make me drunk, will it? I have been traveling all day from gold star to gold star."

"I know," he said. "We got a lot of calls saying you were in Scotland and on the move."

"You know who I am?"

He poured her a beer and wrote her order on a scrap of paper. "We all know, at least those with the gold star."

"What does the gold star mean?" asked Calliope. "You talk like it's an old symbol. I thought it was just for me."

"Why would it be for you?" asked Bruce.

"If you know about me, then you know about this." She held up her fingers and the balls of energy formed. "It seems so easy to do now. This used to be hard."

"The minute you killed the Ancient One, you became our high one, our gold star."

"Are you in that cult on the island?" Calliope got up off the barstool. "I just had a shitty experience so I think I should find another place to eat."

"No, no, please sit." Bruce slid the beer over to her. "I apologize if I was rude when you came in. I thought you were just a lost tourist."

"I was lost until some friends showed me your bar," she said.

"How nice of them, are they loyalists"

"Loyalists? They better be, they're my oracles."

Bruce stopped cold. "You have oracles? Then it really is true."

Calliope nodded, "I have three big fucking crows that will pull your eyes out while cackling."

"I worry less about your birds and more about you, Morning Star."

"Morning Star?

"Yes, some people who follow the Ancient One and the ancient druidic ways prophesized about a star, the sun herself, who would change the world. That's you."

"I'm digging this star motif," she smiled. "If I ever have a superhero costume, I'll make sure it's gold stars."

Bruce walked the paper slip over to the kitchen window, clipped it to a wire, then dinged a bell. "Lucky for you we already know the news. Someone tried to stream a video of your wedding but…well it just vaporized mid-broadcast."

"The wedding," she sighed and took a healthy drink of beer, "what a fucking shit-show that was."

"You don't need a king when you are the queen."

She looked at Bruce and really studied his face: deep red-brown hair and beard, blue eyes, peek-a-boo tattoos on his chest and arms, white Henley with the sleeves pushed up past his elbows. Not bad, she thought, for an older guy.

"So, what brings you here besides the gold star?" He drew a beer for himself and settled in. "I got nowhere to go if you want to talk."

"First, let me ask are you a follower of that thing that wanted to marry me?"

"Just call me an aficionado."

"And how did you become that?" She took another drink.

"I saw it once on my grandfather's fishing boat. Me, my two brothers, and my dad were helping him near the end of the season. Since they found oil off the coast, all the fish had left. We were trying to get back in when a gale hit. It was a terrible squall, I tell ya, missy. That's when the tentacles came up out of the waves and wrapped around the boat."

"Oh my god, what did you do?"

"Dad grabbed the fire ax and chopped clean through a tentacle and it let go. We high-tailed it off the water with that thing coming after us. Just as we pulled to the dock, we didn't even tie her down, it rose up out of the bay. Then, with one smack, the boat and dock were destroyed. If it wasn't for the security lights, it would have killed us, too."

"I was saved by that thing somehow," she said. "I'm looking for help getting back to Old Livonia. You know about that place, right?"

He nodded. "Old Livonia is the worst kept secret. Now it's just a big hole in the ground."

"Yeah, that was me," she said. "I want to go back there. Do you know someone who can help me do that?"

He took a drink and responded as the cook dinged the dinner

bell. He fetched her sandwich, "Why do you want to go there?"

"There is someone there who needs a little payback," said Calliope. She took a bite of the warm sandwich. "This is so good."

"I'm glad you like it, we cure the ham ourselves on the farm about 10 kilometers from here." He noticed her beer was getting empty and drew another. "Do you have a place to stay?"

She shook her head while swallowing. "No, I don't. I was hoping to find a hotel."

"Not really any hotels a respectable young goddess should be staying at," he winked. "Here, this one is on the house."

"Thanks, but I don't want to drink too much. I'm so hungry and tired, I don't want to lose control and do something I would regret. This is a nice place, so I don't think another beer is a good idea."

"What would you do to this place?" he asked. "It would be an improvement. If it burned down, I'd make a lot of money off the insurance. Then I could sell the property to those bastards from London who want a fancy hippy wine bar here."

"Malicious destruction of property?" Calliope winked, "I'm not above that."

"Don't tempt me," added Bruce. "Seriously, what would you do?"

Calliope ate the last bit of her sandwich. "Can I have this jar?"

"The one with the straws in it?" he handed it to her. "Do you want the straws in it?"

"No, I don't want to destroy them. Here, we can just put them on the counter for now." Calliope took the straws out and held the empty jar in her hands. "Just watch."

For many moments, the jar remained empty. Bruce looked on wondering if she was indeed a crazy American who happened to find out what gold stars meant and was fucking around. Then, in the bottom of the jar, a few brilliant plasma balls formed. They split and spread until the entire receptacle was glowing like a streetlight.

"That's really cool," he smiled. "Is that all they do? Glow like that?"

"No, that isn't all they do. They explode. I won't let them explode in here, though. I don't want anyone to get hurt."

"Yeah, I suppose glass would be flying everywhere."

"Exactly," said Calliope has the light faded to emptiness. "Now, imagine that on a scale that fried your dear Ancient One."

"I will certainly watch myself, Morning Star." He looked around the bar as the last drunk customer stumbled out the door. "We can close up now. I would like to offer you accommodations on our farm, if you would allow it." He could see she was unsure. "You can blow us all to hell if we step out of line."

"Promise?" she smiled.

"Promise."

EPIS⊕DE TEN

All That We See or Seem, is But a Dream Within a Dream

"How can they be this far ahead of us?" asked Tiffany from the very small back seat of the Maserati.

"I bet that little witch is hiding them," added Roxette.

"Good, let them be protected," said Janelle. "We will find them eventually. My mind is on Pascal and where our beloved spring has gone. Does it not bother you two that the Pierian Spring left us behind? For the first time in our history?"

"Yes, it does bother me," said Roxette from the passenger side as she watched the dark west Pennsylvania sky go by. "We were not there when it was threatened. It protected itself just like it did when the Hammer killed our sister."

"I will have revenge for that," sneered Tiffany.

"In time, sister," said Janelle as she drove along the empty stretch of highway. "I hope we are on the same road as the children are. There are so many different roads and I think we're following the one on this map," she gestured to the navigation screen dead-center of the dashboard, "well just look at how many roads there are."

"Maybe they left the highway and took the side-roads to avoid detection," conjectured Roxette. "I would do that."

"Essentially, they are all teenagers. I don't have a lot of confidence that they will think that way. They will pick the most direct route to get there as fast as possible. This highway is going to go through many mountain tunnels—and that is a perfect opportunity for an ambush. I hope they are safe until we can catch up to them."

Roxette pointed at a road sign, "The next exit, please. I have to use the bathroom and I am starving."

"We haven't eaten since before the show," added Tiffany. "And what a hell of a show, right?"

"I was speechless," smiled Janelle. "Truly is truly remarkable. I taught her the double knife throw."

"Very nice," said Roxette. "My favorite thing was that the audience ate it up. They thought it was part of the show."

"I don't think she could have gotten away with it any other way. She thought it through. It was a good plan," said Janelle, pulling off the exit. "Wait, sisters…"

As they left the off-ramp and headed toward the bright lights of the truck stop, Janelle slowed cautiously. There were ambulances, a fire truck, and at least three police cruisers. Two bodies were covered with sheets awaiting the coroner.

"It looks like we missed some fun," said Roxette as she rubber-necked through the tinted glass. "I can't see a damn thing. I'm rolling down the window."

Janelle turned off all the power windows from her side, "No, do you want to be seen?" She drove by and back onto the highway. "We don't even know what happened there."

"Seriously, you know it was Truly."

"Unfortunately, I believe you may be right about that." Janelle looked in her rearview mirror. The road was dark except for them. "Look on your phones for another place. I don't know how to work Pascal's stupid GPS."

"Okay, not this exit but the one after looks like it has a lot of stuff," said Tiffany. "Can we actually get out and eat? Or are we eating in the car?"

Janelle glanced back at her younger sister and sighed. "We are in a hurry."

"I'm sure they are in capable hands. I mean they have a goddess and a witch," said Roxette. "We will find them and catch up to them."

"Fine, but it has to be quick."

They continued to gab about Truly's soon-to-be-legendary performance to *Heaven Must Have Sent You*. All conceded that they would never be able to hear the song again without thinking of Truly's final curtain.

The exit on the phone GPS wasn't well-marked and was even less well-lit. Their headlights cast long sinister shadows as the exit wound like a snake downward towards a smaller road. It was a stop light, and a sign on the left berm indicated all the food and gas were a half mile to the left. They turned down the two-lane road and, surely, over the hill was a cluster of closed strip malls, a few fast-food joints, a bright gas station, and a 24-hour diner. Janelle pulled up to the diner and parked in front so they could keep an eye on the car. They walked in and waited at the hostess station.

There was a surprising amount of people in the diner for the late hour and considering the remoteness of the location. Several booths were populated with teenagers hanging out and eating French fries. There were also a few couples softly talking and enjoying some apple pie and coffee.

"Hi, just three tonight?" The young hostess smiled.

Janelle nodded. "Can we sit by the windows so I can keep an eye on my car?"

"That's a nice car," said the hostess. "Follow me. Yeah, we all saw it as soon as you pulled up. I thought a movie star was going to get out. Hey, are you three a singing group or something? You look really cool like *Destiny's Child* or something."

"That is a great compliment, thank you, but we're just normal women. No talent like that, I'm afraid," said Janelle following behind with her sisters. They arrived at a booth that looked directly on the car. "Could I have a cup of coffee and a large glass of water?"

"Anyone else want water or coffee?"

Tiffany scooted in, "I will. Both."

"Me, too," added Roxette also sitting in the booth.

Tiffany waited until the waitress walked away, "This is the whitest restaurant I have ever been in."

Janelle casually looked around, "I was thinking that, too. Remember, we're in Trump country out here."

"Don't even mention that name," said Roxette. "I still have to eat."

Janelle grabbed the dog-eared diner menus from a holder next to the window and distributed them. "Let's eat and get out of here." She took just a second to scan the menu and decided. "Order a chef's salad for me with oil and vinegar on the side." She put the menu back and scooted out of the booth. "I have to use the bathroom."

Her sisters continued to peruse while Janelle located the bathrooms down a hallway beyond the lunch counter. It was a cute place, she thought, with stainless steel stools and tables. It was very nostalgic. As she walked past another table with three guests by an opposite window, Janelle could not help but feel their stares upon her. She made no tip-off that she was aware of them and went into the women's bathroom. Janelle wanted to get a good look at them, for something was off.

She finished and washed her hands, then exited the bathroom. However, on the way back to the table Janelle moved a little slower, scanning the bar side for a reflective surface, a mirror, anything that would offer her a glimpse without letting them see her. Just then, a waitress that was rummaging in the pie case shut the door and Janelle saw a perfect reflection of the customers: a much older man with something wrong with his eyes, a younger woman who wasn't very attractive, and another man. They were strangely dressed in similar dark clothing. Although Janelle only had a few seconds to analyze the reflection, she gathered a lot of information. A final detail made her blood run cold and she focused on getting back to her table.

"Did you order?" she whispered to her sisters.

"Not yet, she brought water and said she would be right back," said Roxette.

"We have to get the food to go," said Janelle with a nuance of anxiety in her voice. "There are Wire agents here. Do not look at them, but they are at the booth next to the bathrooms." Tiffany looked over. "I just said not to look."

"I was looking at the pies," she lied. "I mean how many people will not look when you tell them not to look at something?"

"She's right," agreed Roxette.

Janelle sighed, exasperated. "Here is the waitress."

"Ready to order?"

Janelle began, "This will actually all be take-out. I want a Chef's salad with vinegar and oil on the side."

"We don't have vinegar and oil to go. We have Italian and ranch."

Janelle wrinkled her nose distastefully, "Italian will do."

"And I will have the chicken tenders basket," said Tiffany.

"Me, too," added Roxette.

"That was easy," the waitress smiled. "You the girls with the car? We were talking about it. It's so awesome."

"Thank you," said Janelle. "Will it take long? We have to get back on the road. Our mother is sick, and we are driving to see her."

"Are you sisters? I should have seen the resemblance." She put her pen in her apron, "I'll put this in right now. Shouldn't take long." She was off.

Roxette leaned in close as did the other two. "What makes you think they are the Wire?"

"They are all dressed strangely," started Janelle. "But they all have the same stainless-steel watches."

"Ah, the kind like they used to try and kill Truly," said Tiffany.

"We can take them if they start anything," said Roxette.

"We are not starting any fights with anyone, do you hear? They do not know who we are. We are not gods or oracles so they would have no clue that we are also pursuing them. We will just get our food and go. In fact, you two stay here and I will go fill up the tank across the street. Pay for the food and meet me outside if you get it before I'm done. I will pick you up." They nodded. "Good."

The waitress returned and intercepted Janelle, "I'm sorry did you want anything to drink?"

"No, I am going to get gas over there and I will get some sodas," said Janelle, trying not to be rude but desperate to leave.

"Okay," smiled the waitress and went to another table.

Janelle rushed out of the diner, started the car, and drove across the broad intersection of local roads and highway service drives to the gas station. Just as she was pulling up to the pump, a pickup truck pulled up to the other side. They were separated by the concrete island that supported the gas pumps. Do not make any eye contact, Janelle told herself as she walked past to go pay the cashier. She made a mental note that a credit card would be rather convenient if they were going to be living in the outside world again.

"That is a sweet car!" exclaimed the teenage boy working the register behind his bulletproof glass.

"Thank you," she said. "I need $40 on that pump. I don't know the number."

He looked out the window then back at her again. "You sure?"

"Why? What do you mean?"

"I mean, that guy in the pickup truck just went over to your pump and swiped his card. He is filling your tank."

Surprised, she looked out the window. "He is?"

Indeed, that was the case. The tall man wore a distressed denim jacket that was paint-stained. He had on black, well-worn work boots and a ballcap turned backward. She couldn't get a good read on his face, though, the lights were casting deceptive shadows.

Janelle sprinted out the door to intercept him. "Excuse me, you don't have to do that."

He smiled as she approached, and she was slightly punched in the face by his handsomeness: deep dimples beneath a neatly trimmed brown beard with touches of nutmeg, blue eyes brighter than the overhead LEDs, a solid frame with shoulders that spanned beyond his small waist.

"Sorry, I saw you were alone, and you went in to pay," he said. "It's not safe for a lady to be out this late. I thought it would be a nice gesture. I'm sorry if I offended you."

Janelle sighed, taking in the onslaught of sudden information from the situation. "No, I am sorry. Thank you for the kindness. I shall pay it forward the next time I get a chance." He wasn't coming off as a creep, but it was an unusual gesture. "My sisters are in the diner getting food."

"Nice, it's a good place for a cheap meal," he said. He topped off her tank and replaced the nozzle. Then he walked over to his own truck and swiped his card. "That's a beautiful car. You don't want to leave that unattended, so I was trying to help you stay in it, that's all."

"I appreciate it, sincerely," she said.

He grinned and a slight laugh of amusement escaped his lips. "You don't sound from around here."

"I'm not. We're driving to see our parents," Janelle recalled the previous excuse and figured it was just as good as any at the moment.

"I work at a body shop," he referenced his own appearance. "I just got off. Totally backed up with work."

"I bet you get to see a lot of nice cars," she said while opening the driver's side door.

"Not like this," he said. He pumped gallon after gallon into his truck. "What's your name? I'm Wil, nice to meet you."

"Nice to meet you, too, Wil." She got in and closed the door, but quickly rolled down the window as not to seem rude. "I have to go pick up my sisters now."

"You never said your name?" Wil seemed a little disappointed.

"It's Mary," she said.

"If you're ever in this area again, maybe I will run into you again. Not late night at a creepy gas station."

Janelle loved his smile, "You never know."

She rolled up the window, started the car, and drove back across to the diner. Her sisters were standing outside, giggling and grinning. Roxette climbed into the backseat and allowed Tiffany the legroom of the passenger side for the next leg. Janelle spied and cut her eyes at them while they continued to whisper and giggle.

"What is so funny?" she asked as they got back on the road.

"Even from here, we could see you talking to that man," said Tiffany. "He was pretty. At least from here."

"You both are being silly."

"Are we?" asked Tiffany. "We saw him pumping your gas."

There was a long pause. Then, Janelle grinned, too. "He was pretty. And he paid for and pumped that gas. Why can't I find a man like that? Seriously?"

"Amen, sister," Tiffany dug into her take-out bag and snatched a chicken finger.

Fletcher lay on his bed simply staring at the tin tiles of his ceiling. He wondered who put them there originally. There were rumors about the building itself, but he knew history was a liar. A penny fell onto his chest. He sat up.

"That's for your thoughts," said Oni who was floating nearby.

"Where did you get a penny?" Fletcher still stared at the ceiling.

"I'm full of surprises," said Oni and he settled onto Fletcher's chest. He tickled his god's nose with his tassel-like tail. "Come on, let's do something. It's boring around here."

"You were the one who wanted to be un-banished," smiled Fletcher. "I wasn't thinking about anything, really. I was wondering who put those tin tiles on the ceiling."

Oni scoffed. "That's what you are wasting time on?"

"I just need a mental break for a bit, you know. There is so much going on—so much going wrong."

"Why are you so convinced it is going wrong?" Oni undulated in the air to remain vertical.

"I don't know," sighed Fletcher. "It doesn't feel right, that's for sure. You've been down in the Underworld where it's relatively peaceful."

"The Underworld peaceful?" Oni popped his tongue. "Seriously, you think that?"

"Yeah, I mean its smoother, no hassles."

"Do you know why that is?" asked Oni, but he was ready with the answer. "You're the god damn Prince of Shadows. Do you think anything would go wrong for you? Your father is Pluto."

"I guess you have a point," sighed Fletcher.

"I bet if you stopped with this human disguise your third eye would see so much more."

"My third eye sees just fine. That's what causes most of my trouble."

"Because it won't lie to you like your human eyes do?"

Fletcher sat up. "I don't have time for this." He got up, "I am going crazy waiting for things to happen. I don't know where Calliope is. That's my fault. PJ is in the Underworld. That's my fault. Carmen has turned to the dark side, that's my fault."

"Yeah, that one really is all you."

Fletcher gritted his teeth and his jaw muscle jumped. "You're not helping."

Just then, Ray tapped on the semi-open door. "Sorry, I didn't mean to interrupt your nap."

"I wasn't getting any sleep," he glared at Oni, "some creature won't shut up."

"That hurts my feelings," pouted Oni.

Fletcher rolled his eyes, "What is it?"

"It's not on the news, but there were a few things on the short-wave radio we hooked up."

"We have a short-wave radio?" asked Fletcher.

Ray nodded, "There is like everything in this place. It's like twenty garage sales all in one around here. Nash found it."

"He is industrious, that one." Oni zoomed over to Ray, "Let's go."

"You," said Fletcher with authority, "not you. You are too distracting."

"What am I supposed to do, then?" whined Oni.

"Go find Cleo and bother her."

Oni zoomed, "She's doing yoga, and I don't want to bother her."

Fletcher was exhausted, "If you can stay quiet and out of the way…"

"I can do that!" Oni whizzed one lap around the ceiling. "Let's go."

Fletcher followed Ray, who was followed by a giddy Oni, and they went to the improvised battle room. Nash was attending some new equipment that had been added to the array. There was an old stereo receiver, another TV, and a PC.

"What have you got?" asked Fletcher.

"A lot of chatter about the border with Mexico," Nash answered, concentrating on the static coming over the monitor speakers rigged through the receiver. "They keep saying '*todos estan*'."

"All are…" Fletcher translated. "All are what?"

"If you didn't take our phones, I could be helping you now," said Ray with Oni hovering near his shoulder. "We could be looking for everyone, you know?"

"It's too big of a risk," said Fletcher.

"Shh," hushed Nash.

Ellos estan muertos! Ellos estan muertos!

"All the men are dead?" questioned Fletcher. "I'm not the greatest at Spanish, but isn't that what he is saying?"

"Can I use the computer?" Asked Ray. "You can type that into any translation program. But I am sure if you let me use the internet, I can find out some more info."

"Fine," Fletcher walked over and typed in the password, "all yours."

"Let's see..." Ray got busy searching. He logged on to YouTube. "Let's see if there are any videos or something." He typed in some terms, but the results were not helpful. "Do you have anything else that you heard?"

"No, just what I said," answered Nash.

"Okay let's think about this," said Ray. "Professor, what are some of the things you know about Carmen that may help."

"She speaks Spanish, for one thing."

"Spanish, okay that may be something. She speaks Spanish and what we heard was in Spanish." Ray typed in a few more words, "How about Mexico or Florida, where else do they speak a lot of Spanish."

"Like everywhere," sighed Nash.

The room went silent. "Hey, guys, I think our search just got a little easier," said Fletcher as he grabbed the TV remote and turned up the sound.

The country is on high alert after another powerful and mysterious terrorist attack. This time in south Texas at an infamous border crossing. For years, immigrants have snuck across the Rio Grande river. Most get caught and returned. But not today. Leaked phone footage on the Internet shows an attack similar to the one on Washington D.C.

Experts will not comment if it is the same group or individual responsible, but video suggests it may be one and the same. And the weapon they are using is not like anything anyone has seen before.

Only fuzzy images of the attacker have surfaced. If you have any information leading to the identification of the person, please contact your local authorities.

"Thank you, news teams," sighed Nash. "So does this mean we're going to Texas?"

"No, not yet," said Fletcher. "I don't think she will be there anymore. Let's see what happens next with Carmen. She seems to have an agenda."

"What agenda, killing a lot of people with little effort as possible?" asked Nash.

"There's got to be more to it," he said, studying the videos that were playing on the news. "Can you find these on the Internet?"

"Easy," said Ray. "I guess we should have just checked the news sites."

"There's going to be a pattern, believe me." Fletcher looked at the phone videos with the others, "It doesn't make sense yet, but it will. She never does anything that doesn't make sense to her."

Ray was still on the computer, and a news story popped up. "What is this?" He pointed at the screen, "Look at this story."

"What is it?" asked Fletcher, peering over his shoulder.

Nash also looked, "It's a satellite loop. What are we looking at?"

Ray read: "Satellite images have captured what is thought to believe a meteor hitting the atmosphere over northern Scotland, resulting in a brilliant explosion. According to this, it happened in a remote area and there are no reports of damage or injuries."

"That is awfully bright and looks like something I have seen before," commented Nash.

"This is fascinating, but we should get back to the task of finding Carmen," said Fletcher.

"Right," agreed Ray and he logged off the computer. "Meteors hit the Earth all the time."

Cleo sat in the lotus position in the small room off the main tattoo studio. It had always been her room since they moved the operation here in 1938. It wasn't a tattoo shop then, and none of the buildings were connected. Professor Fletcher and Nash carved out the entire outpost inside all the buildings once he was able to buy them up. During the war it was an easy purchase.

The door was closed. She didn't want anything to do with their Scooby Doo operation out in the main room. They weren't going to be able to find Carmen by monitoring the news and stupid shortwave radio. Carmen was the Hammer now, and she was learning how to wield it fiercely. Cleo didn't want to be anywhere near when they found her.

"Focus," she whispered to herself.

Cleo inhaled deeply, taking in the fragrance of the eucalyptus and lavender candles that were the only illumination in the room. She sat erect but not stiff, focusing on her posture. The breaths slowed and deepened. In and out. In and out.

Her yoga mat was in the middle of her tiny room and her twin bed was against the wall. Her eyes drifted from the authentic paintings from some of the great masters. She had been collecting them all these centuries. She wouldn't be surprised if they were worth a small fortune. It was a shame that all those great artists were dead, but at least she had a piece of them.

Screw it, she thought and concentrated on her task. Cleo began with her poses: first she lay prone on the mat in her child's pose, then moved to planks. She followed this with her favorite, cobra pose, for it released all the tension in her back and hamstrings. The routine continued and she became more limber for some advanced poses.

Cleo then lay on her back to execute her routine. Her head and shoulders were in a deep shadow cast by the flickering candles, but her torso and legs were not. The first pose was the bridge to further loosen up. Repeatedly, she lifted her hips to relieve the tightness, held it, then lowered back down to the mat.

After many repetitions, she lay to simply rest. Cleo put her palm on her diaphragm to connect with her breathing.

Suddenly, the candles flickered as an icy breeze, more like someone opening a door during the dead of winter, chilled her. Two hands came up out of the shadows. One covered her mouth so she couldn't scream for help. Cleo struggled and kicked her legs violently. One knocked over the small table with the candles, enlarging the shadows around her. Then with a swift strong tug, the arms pulled her into the shadows and away from this world.

The journey was swift and over as quickly as it began. Cleo stood on the porch of an old house, and she was not alone. Behind her, someone held Cleo's hands, but her mouth was no longer covered.

"Let me go!" she shouted.

"Stop struggling," said Carmen. "I brought you to your mistress." She shoved her through the doorway.

Cleo fell to the dried, knotted floorboards. "What are you doing? This is crazy!"

"Cleo?" it was Nemesis' voice.

"Nemesis?" Cleo forgot all about Carmen and turned. It was her goddess coming to her, "How? Oh, I'm so glad you're not hurt."

Nemesis knelt by Cleo, "I'm fine, but what about you?" She turned her glare towards Carmen, her eyes swirling with crystal-blue energy. "You will pay for this."

"I don't know about that," said Carmen. "I found a prison for a god, and I have brought you one of your most precious possessions: your oracle. You two can pass time for eternity."

Nemesis pulled Cleo close, "You're safe now. Don't worry."

"Oh, you aren't safe now and you should worry," smiled Carmen through her sugar skull makeup. "I'm just getting started."

The farmhouse was not what Calliope expected. She prepared herself for some dilapidated shack where Bruce probably killed all the local virgins, but she was still up for an adventure. After all, he ran a bar called The Gold Star, and there was a gold star nailed onto the front door, what could go wrong?

"It's a little rustic," said Bruce while he threw his backpack on the sofa. "My mother died two years ago and my father just before that. This was a full working farm. We had cows and sheep, and too many chickens to count."

"I'm sorry," said Calliope.

"Don't worry," his accent was quite thick that she had to focus on his words to understand them. "I think I will sell it soon. I don't have time to work here like I should. I sold off a great lot of the herd and used it to buy the bar."

"Planning for the future?" asked Calliope.

"Planning for the future," he smiled. "Fancy a little whiskey? I know American girls like their frilly sweet flower drinks."

"This girl is not like that," said Calliope. "I may need an ice cube or two."

He laughed. "My mum could only drink it cold, too." He moved to the quaint kitchen area and fetched a glass with a couple of ice cubes. Then he pulled a bottle out of the nearby cabinet and another rock glass. "This is actually distilled around here. It isn't for sale…" he poured two healthy portions, "…meaning it is rather potent."

"I won't tell if you don't," said Calliope. She looked around the décor, "It's really charming."

"That's a nice way of saying crap," he laughed.

"No, the nice way to say that is to call everything 'antique' or 'shabby chic.'" She watched him pour her drink over the ice cubes. "Thanks."

"Not a problem," he smiled. "It's not often I get to have a drink with a god."

"I think that is stretching things," she said, taking the drink. "I'm just a girl who happens to have a unique talent."

He laughed and held his glass high. "Here's to women with unique talents."

"Cheers!" she clinked his glass, and they drank. "Wow you weren't lying." She shook her head like a wet dog and wrinkled her nose.

"You know it isn't going to get any easier for you now," he said while refilling his glass. Hers still had half, "You will not be welcomed by loyalists to the Ancient One."

"Are you a loyalist? You have a gold star on your door."

"I am not a loyalist to one god. I am a loyalist to whom I believe is real. I believe there are a lot of gods, big and small, I think all of us with gold stars think that. But some get their entire identity from the god or religion they follow whether it is real or just bullshit."

"Is it real or just bullshit to you?" she asked.

"Eh, putting me on the spot, are ya?"

Calliope finished the last swallow of whiskey and pushed the empty glass towards Bruce. "It's a fair question. I used to go to Sunday school, and I thought I believed all of it, too. I like the sentiments that were taught. You know, be nice to your neighbors and don't kill people."

"Those are good, I like them, too. But are they realistic? I mean, have you ever met a human being that is that selfless?"

"Only selfish. Always after their own personal bliss regardless of who gets hurt." Her eyes drifted to the window. "It seems like guys want nothing from me but a piece of ass, or…" she popped a few plasma balls on her nail tips, "…what you can do for them." Then she looked him square in the eye, "Do you want anything from me, Bruce?"

"Not a thing," he said and pushed back a refilled glass. "I am up for an adventure, though. It's boring in these parts. Now that you have blown the Ancient One to oblivion, I do believe the adventures will be coming to you."

"Probably, but I'm not really interested in anything new just yet. I have a few scores to settle—then maybe."

"Ah, the goddess has scores to settle. Pity them folks."

"Pity them folks is right."

The fog hung in every valley of western Pennsylvania. It was well past midnight as they approached the region of the Pennsylvania turnpike that contained several long, deep tunnels going beneath the mountains. As Kendall drove along the empty turnpike, he seemed oblivious, but Truly was troubled. She looked in the back seat and everyone was asleep.

"You okay?" asked Kendall. "You can put on some music if you want. I was keeping it off because everyone was asleep."

"Something seems off to me," she said. Truly looked at the GPS on the monitor on the dash. "Tunnels. I hate tunnels."

"We are about to go through a lot of them," said Kendall. "I remember as a kid, we would drive this road to get to my grandmother's house in NEPA—that's short for Northeastern Pennsylvania."

"I'm from Pennsylvania, I know where NEPA is," she said.

"Sorry," Kendall put his eyes back on the road, "I don't know you that well. I don't know where you grew up and shit like that." He pointed at a sign, "It says fog area. I wonder if it will get foggy?"

"I thought you said you remembered these roads? It is totally a fog area. It will creep up on you, so keep your eyes sharp." There was a humming in Truly's ear as Mico fluttered to her shoulder from the dashboard. "What?"

"Are you talking to your bird or to me?"

"Not you," said Truly. She looked out the window. "There is the fog. See it? Maybe we should pull over until it clears."

"That could take until morning until the sun burns it off," said Kendall. "We would lose so much time, and we don't know where those Wire assholes are. I say we keep driving." He smiled, "First tunnel is coming up." He pointed at a large sign with flashing yellow lights that could barely cut through the fog.

They really didn't look like warning lights at all, more resembling colored, underwater lights in a cloudy hot tub. As they got closer, Truly could see the sign warning about flammable liquids and explosives. She wished she had some of those.

"Look at how bright it is," said Kendall as they approached the tunnel.

It was more like an alien runway, thought Truly. The elongated sodium lights on the high poles burned against the fog. The visibility was only a few hundred feet in front of them. They couldn't really see if there were cars in front or approaching from behind. To Truly it felt like they were on a jet that was taxiing for takeoff as the lights streamed past.

"Just take it slow," she said.

"There won't be any fog in the tunnel, so you can relax."

"I'm never relaxed."

As Kendall predicted, the tunnel was fog-free. It was clear and well-lit. There were no other vehicles with them in the tunnel, nor did they see any ahead or behind. Mico buzzed in Truly's ear making her more agitated. They were speaking to her, but only Truly could understand. Kendall reminded himself that Truly was a god and Mico was her oracle, and they shared a language all their own.

"See we're coming out of it now, and it looks less foggy on this side of the mountain."

They emerged from the tunnel. Kendall was purposely driving beneath the speed limit because visibility was still treacherous, but the fog had indeed lifted about fifteen feet above the road. Then, in the distance, they saw a row of blinking yellow lights on a barricade blocking the road.

"Fuck, the road is closed up ahead," he said.

"No, it's not. Stop the car." Truly smoothed her hair back with her hands and put it in a ponytail holder. "I will check it out."

As the vehicle stopped, it woke Sarah. "Are we stopping?"

"We aren't getting out," said Truly. The others woke. "All of you stay alert and stay in the car. You understand?"

"What's going on?" asked Allison groggily.

"We're stopping," said Sarah.

"What the fuck," snapped Poppy. "I'm trying to sleep." She opened her eyes and sat up. "What's that in the road?"

"I don't know," said Truly. It looks like construction or something. I will check it out."

"I'm going with you," said Poppy.

"No, you stay in here with everyone else. If something happens to me, you are their only protection."

"If something happens to you?" asked Kendall. "Your little bird had a divination, didn't they?"

Truly ignored him. "Poppy, do you got it? Kill them all if something happens to me."

The young witch smiled, "You can count on me."

"Okay," sighed Truly, and she reached for the door handle.

She got out. Mico whizzed by and up into the fog. Truly assessed the situation: the fog deck was above the road; visibility was relatively clear; seven or eight shadowy figures stood about 300 feet away in front of the barricade. They were not law enforcement.

"Move that so we can get by!" yelled Truly. "I won't ask you twice."

"You are in no position to demand anything," said someone, obviously in charge.

The phalanx of shadows walked slowly towards the vehicle. Inside, they were all staring out the windshield. As the strangers walked closer, some would stop every few yards or so until they were staggered in a pattern and not in a line. They drew their weapons.

"You can come with us alive, or you can come in body bags."

Truly took inventory of their positions. Her heightened senses could hear heartbeats, breathing, even the trembling of nervous hands. They all smelled of testosterone and anxiety, none of them were female. They had to be part of the same ones that attacked them previously.

"We know who you are," the man called out.

"Good, then you know what's about to happen," answered Truly. "You can't win. This is your last chance to move the barricade."

A ripple of laughter went through them. "Kill them all. Especially anyone in that SUV."

Before a gun could be fired one of the men fell silently to the pavement. The one behind him also fell. One of the men went to check on them, then stood up and started to scream something.

"They have a hummingbird assassin! Take cov…" He fell dead as Mico burst through his neck and darted back up into the fog.

"Fire!" shouted the leader.

Truly could smell the bullet heating the air as it left the gun's chamber. She predicted where it would go and moved ahead of it in time. The men stood like statues as she sped up, drawing her knife in the process. To them, she was a flash and then gone. The remaining men had fired their guns at the same time, aiming for the SUV. Truly could not see the bullets to predict where they would go, but she could stop any more from being fired. She flashed forward predicting where the men would be in five seconds. Her blade sliced through what seemed like three throats simultaneously before she stopped. They were all dead, but the bullets headed for the windshield full of eager bystanders. Dread filled Truly, she couldn't stop them.

Suddenly they impacted into an unseen shield and fell to the pavement. Poppy stood on top of the SUV, hands and eyes glowing with magic. Truly raised her hands to her face and sighed with relief.

"You're welcome!" shouted Poppy.

"Thank you!" said Truly.

Then Poppy narrowed her eyes at one of the men in the darkness. He was on his knees and aimed his gun at Truly. He wasn't able to get the shot off for Mico burst through one side of his skull and out the other. The man slumped and collapsed with his mates.

"Jesus Christ!" Kendall got out. "What the fuck!"

"It was a trap," said Truly. "They were going to kill us all."

"The Wire," said Poppy from the top of the SUV.

Just then, they heard a car coming through the tunnel. Its lights shined onto the dead men in the road just in front of the barricade, looking like bowling pins brought down with a strike. Truly readied her knife, there could be no witnesses -- innocent or guilty.

"Wait!" Screamed Kendall. "Don't! We know them!"

Pascal's Maserati screeched to a stop. Janelle scrambled out as did Roxette and Tiffany. They looked at the dead men in the middle of the Pennsylvania Turnpike.

"They tried to block the road," said Truly.

"Nice to see you, too," said Janelle sarcastically. "What happened?"

"Like I said they tried to block the road," Truly put the knife away. "I believe they are part of the Wire."

"I would say so," commented Roxette. "We have to get out of here."

"Wait," said Kendall, "shouldn't you be at the car wash?"

Janelle seemed heartbroken. "The Pierian Spring relocated without us. We are guardians with nothing to guard. We must find the fountain wherever it is in the world."

"Why do you have Pascal's car?" asked Poppy as she climbed down off the roof, onto the hood, and plopped onto the pavement.

"He is missing," said Janelle. "We don't know where he is or what happened to him."

"Do you think the Wire got him?" posited Sarah. "I hope not. I don't know what I would do."

"I don't think he's dead, but I don't know where he is," said Janelle.

"We have to get going," said Truly. "Everyone back inside."

"What about all these…these…" Allison could not finish her sentence.

"…Dead bodies?" Poppy finished for her. "They will get over it. Come on, before any more of them come along."

They got back inside while Truly walked over to speak with Janelle and her sisters. "We could use you."

Janelle gestured to the carnage on the pavement, "Looks like you handled them just fine. What do you need us for?"

"They almost died tonight because I couldn't be in five places at once. Poppy saved them."

"You are in good hands, then."

"Do you want to find your fountain?" asked Truly. "I don't know this Fletcher guy we're going to see in Detroit, but he may be able to help you."

"He's not the goddamn Wizard of Oz," snapped Roxette.

"Truly's right, though," Janelle turned to her sisters. "He may have information that can help us. He was once close with Pascal, he may be able to help find him, too." The sisters nodded reluctantly. "Okay, we will go with you, but we will not stay once we have a direction to follow. We are bound to the spring and to protect it above all else."

Truly started walking back to the SUV, "Race you to Detroit."

Janelle and her sisters got back in the Maserati and joined the SUV, spinning out on the pavement.

Pascal wandered in the trees and meadows of the grotto. It made no sense to him. He was quite familiar with the Pierian Spring and its mysteries, but this seemed a bit much. He lost track of how many hours he had been walking in the trees that seemed to be neither thickening nor getting more sparse. Every now and again, Pascal would come upon a meadow with an open sky, but as he crossed it to enter it turned out to be trees again—it all started to seem like the same maze. He came to another opening after walking for what seemed hours, but he really didn't know.

"This is getting very old," he said to himself. The edge of the meadow shimmered like a heat mirage. "Hello?"

There was no answer. There were no birds or butterflies. Everything alive seemed to be non-existent. The only movement was coming from the wind. He sat on the ground and then lay on his back. Pascal simply stared into the sky at the puffy white clouds dotting the clear blue.

That cloud looks like Ireland.

The song lyrics from a Kate Bush song haunted his mind as he watched the clouds ambling by.

Come on blow it a kiss, now.

"I'm looking at the Big Sky," a woman's lilting soprano voice played on the wind. "I'm looking at the Big Sky now. I'm looking at the Big Sky. You never really understood me. You never really tried."

Pascal sat bolt upright. Who sang that? Who knew that song was in his brain? He stood. "Who's there?"

There was silence and it seemed like the wind ceased blowing. The leaves stopped singing. Then in the distance, where there was a tree line when he lay down, upon rising it was a pergola ringed with trees and flowers. There was a figure simply sitting on some rocks by a murmuring spring.

"Hey!" Pascal waved his hands and took off running towards the person. "Don't leave! Hold on!"

He covered the distance rather swiftly. Pascal slowed as he approached. There was a young woman who couldn't be more than twenty sitting there. She looked out of place, out of time, with pinned up red curls that fell like a waterfall down the side of her dove-white skin. Behind her exposed ear was a bright pink flower. Even from the distance he was, Pascal could see her green eyes clearly. And her dress was out-of-time as well. He had seen the style before but only in old photographs of Hollywood and in Alberto Vargas paintings.

"Hi," he said.

"Hello," she replied. "It's such a beautiful day."

"Yes, it is." He studied her. "I heard you singing the song that was in my head. How did you do that?"

She started to sing again in a spellbindingly clear, perfect-pitched coloratura soprano: "They look down. At the ground. Missing. But I never go in now."

"Yes, that song. It's one of my favorites," he smiled. "I thought of it just now when I was looking at the clouds."

She nodded, "I heard you."

"But I didn't sing it out loud," he confessed.

Her smile was radiant, "I could hear it still. I don't know what else to say."

"What's your name?" he asked.

"Come and sit down with me," she avoided the question. "You're the first person I've ever met."

I don't know what you mean. Are there other people here? Is this still the Pierian Spring? You can never be too sure of anything these days."

She drew her slender white fingers across the surface, gentler than a swan's wingtip. "I think so." She looked up and off to the right as if she were trying to remember something, "It sounds about right."

"The others that you have seen—are there three black women? They are the guardians of the fountain."

"No," she shook her head. "It was a blonde young man. I like him a lot, but I never got his name."

"You never said yours," reminded Pascal. "I am Pascal. It's a pleasure to meet you."

"I'm Betty," she smiled. "It is a pleasure to meet you, too."

"Such a classic name," he smiled. "I love it."

"Thank you," said Betty. "I don't think I have ever heard the name Pascal before. It was Pascal, right?"

He nodded. "An old family name. My father was Pascal. My grandfather, too."

"That's wonderful!" her laugh was a tinkle of crystal.

"I'm glad you find my name so delightful," he said. "What are the names of any of the other people you think you may know here?"

"I don't know any of their names," she said. "At least not the names that would come out of their mouth. You know, names given to them by their mother or father."

"Who named you?"

"No one," said Betty. "I remember someone asking me my name, and it was just there: Betty."

"Was it this blonde fellow you talked about?"

"Yes, he is such a sweet soul."

"How long have you been here?" he asked. "Is there any food? I haven't eaten in a long time. I don't even know how long."

Her smile faded as she tried to recall if she had an answer for Pascal. "Food. I don't know. But if you are thirsty, the spring is delicious."

"Maybe in a little while," Pascal flashed back to the chaos when he first tasted the magic water.

"You want to see something really wonderful?" asked Betty.

"Sure," replied Pascal.

Betty knelt to the ground in her pencil-straight red skirt that stopped high on her thigh, and a corset-like top that accentuated her bosom. She had bright red matching pumps that coordinated with it all. Then with no effort or resistance, she sank her hands deep into the soil like it was warm pudding. Out she pulled a glowing purple crystal orb.

"Isn't it gorgeous?"

He could not trust what he saw and thought the grotto was playing tricks on him. "What is it?"

"I don't know, but I can reach inside and get things like this if I want them."

He knelt down and inspected the earth where Betty had just pulled the sphere. It was solid. He touched it with a flat hand as well. Still, there was no purchase.

"Can you put it back?" he asked.

"Sure," she said and pushed it back inside the earth from where it came. "See."

He sighed. "Betty, I don't know where I am or what I'm doing here. I thought it was the grotto of the Pierian Spring, but my mind is a little foggy. Maybe I am dead."

"You're where you're supposed to be, I'm sure of it." She stood back up. "I don't know where I am either, but I'm not scared or worried. I feel fantastic. And I'm glad you're here with me."

"I think I am thirsty now," said Pascal.

Pascal walked over to the fountain, cupped his hands, and lifted the water to his lips. It was so frosty and refreshing. His mind swirled and some of the fog was lifting. Perhaps it was the influence of the grotto that was disorienting him, but now it was better.

"I remember now," he said.

"Great," said Betty. "Now tell me all about it."

ACKNOWLEDGEMENTS

Grateful and Deserved Thanks

I dedicate this novel to the support of my nurses and doctors at the University of Pennsylvania as I fought severe sepsis for months during the late summer and fall of 2021. There were more than a few moments when I wasn't sure if I would make it, but I still wrote in notebooks while I endured tests, CT scans, an IV pole full of antibiotics, and vampiric phlebotomists stealing my blood in the middle of the night.

My husband Cody was there, indispensable, taking care of our lives and our furry babies—never complaining once when he had to help nurse me back to health at home. I still wrote all-the-while. I was thankful that I could escape into my fantasy worlds and forget that I had a drain tube sticking out of my back, drawing off toxins and infection from around my mysteriously bleeding kidney. I am so fucking blessed that I met this amazing human being—and he is all mine.

I also need to thank Alex, Allison, Emily, and Miriam at Fractured Mirror Publishing for believing in this strange tale that is still unfolding in unexpected and delightful ways.

ABOUT THE AUTHOR

STEVEN LEE CLIMER is a born creative and works in the written, visual, and aural arts. He has been writing fantasy, horror, and science fiction for kids of all ages, for over 30 years. He is the author of 15 novels, including the award-winning *Dream Thieves*, and *Demonesque,* which was optioned for a feature film.

His short stories have appeared in print and online publications in North America and the UK. Steven is also an accomplished acrylic and oil painter, and when not writing and painting, Steven composes chill EDM music under the name SugarBuzz. His music can be experienced on Spotify, Apple Music, iHeartRadio, and Amazon Music. He believes there are different voices and moods for each creative medium—like family harmony. He lives with the love of his life in Philadelphia, and they are the proud dads of a porkie named Rocky and two cats.

KEEP READING FOR A PREVIEW OF

SHADOWWORK

BOOK #3 IN THE BLOODSTREAM SAGA BY
STEVEN LEE CLIMER

An excerpt from

SHADOWWORK

Book 3 in the Bloodstream Saga

Compeer White Eyes stirred extra cream and sugar in his coffee as was his habit. He sat with his fellow compeers Benedicta and Franz in a diner along the highway in the economically-devastated area of eastern Ohio between Youngstown and Cleveland. It was inconspicuous but not too far away from the highway tunnel of western Pennsylvania where the massacre of Wire agents lay on the pavement.

"It's not on the news yet," commented Benedicta, watching White Eyes stirring his coffee and staring at it with his cataract-dead eyes. "You're going to kill yourself with diabetes by putting that much sugar in your coffee."

White Eyes put the spoon down and took the coffee cup. "Thank you for your concern, but my long-term health is irrelevant because none of us may survive what is unfolding."

"What do you mean?" asked Franz.

White Eyes sipped his coffee, savored the taste, then took another before setting the cup down again. "I love diner coffee, don't you?" Franz and Benedicta traded furtive glances. "Ah, you are concerned and looking at each other. Remember, I can see quite a lot even though I am blind."

"Can you blame us?" commented Franz. "I mean, how many agents died on that highway last night? 10, 11, 12?"

"The amount doesn't matter," he said dismissively. "Remember what I told you?"

"Send in your pawns first, then analyze the data," said Compeer Benedicta. "I don't find sacrificing our personnel just to see how they are killed."

"You two are still so foolish," White Eyes said. "None of us could have stood a chance against this new…" he paused to select the correct description, "…god. Is she *skyborne, earthborne, starborne*? There are many critical elements in play now, numerous new gods are showing up. More than I can keep straight in my mind's eye. Then beyond this new creature who can so easily kill our agents, the Hammer has returned."

"I thought the Hammer was a myth created by us long ago to keep people in line," mused Benedicta.

White Eyes cast his cloudy, disturbing eyes in her direction. "No, the Hammer is very real. She is a devastating force that only comes around once in a great, great while. The last Hammer to visit earth was in ancient times."

"What is the Hammer?" asked Franz.

"Pure bloodstream energy that is wielded by a female to balance reality—keep the bloodstream of the universe balanced. If it tips too far off center, chaos can take hold and become like a snowball rolling down a mountain." He sipped his coffee. "I think we missed the start of the snowball."

The server brought their breakfasts and set them on the table with the bill. "Anything else for you?"

"We are fine, thank you," said White Eyes. She left them alone. "My vision is overwhelmed with the surging emergence of *newbornes.*"

I am confused," confessed Franz. "Is this Hammer a god? What about this person who can wipe out our agents in a matter of minutes? And what about the newbornes we have been chasing all over Philadelphia and Detroit?"

"It's difficult to keep it all straight," added Benedicta as she began to eat her eggs and bacon.

"Do not worry yourselves with that, you just do as I direct, and we will be fine. Your talents will be challenged in the near future, so make sure you stay alert." White Eyes tasted his omelet. "This is cold."

Franz stood and flagged down the server, "My grandfather's eggs are cold. Take them back and fix it."

"I'm sorry about that," she whisked the plate away. "Be right back."

Benedicta took out a tiny notebook from her pocket and a pen. "I have started keeping track of things because I am getting confused."

"It will get worse before it gets better," said White Eyes. "Not only must we contend with these two wild cards, we still must contain Phineas Fletcher's proteges."

"We can't get a line on them, though. They seem to slip through our fingers every time," said Franz.

White Eyes laughed. "We let them slip so we can follow them. We need to study them more, and they are young. They will slip-up, make a big mistake and that will be our opening."

The server returned with a fresh, steaming omelet, "Sorry about that."

"Don't worry about it," White Eyes said. "There are much bigger things to worry about in life than some cold eggs."

www.ingramcontent.com/pod-product-compliance
Lightning Source LLC
Chambersburg PA
CBHW021141190726
48288CB00008B/2768

9 781737 920779